WILLIAM L. DAWSON

AMERICAN

Composers

For a list of books in the series, please see our
website at www.press.uillinois.edu.

William L. Dawson

Gwynne Kuhner Brown

UNIVERSITY OF ILLINOIS PRESS
Urbana, Chicago, and Springfield

Publication of this book was
supported by a grant from the
Henry and Edna Binkele Classical
Music Fund.

Library of Congress Cataloging-in-Publication Data
Names: Brown, Gwynne Kuhner, 1973– author.
Title: William L. Dawson / Gwynne Kuhner Brown.
Description: Urbana : University of Illinois Press, 2024. |
    Series: American composers | Includes bibliographical
    references and index.
Identifiers: LCCN 2024003637 (print) | LCCN
    2024003638 (ebook) | ISBN 9780252045967
    (hardcover) | ISBN 9780252088063 (paperback) |
    ISBN 9780252047145 (ebook)
Subjects: LCSH: Dawson, William L. (William Levi),
    1899–1990. | African-American composers—
    Biography. | Composers—United States—Biography.
    | LCGFT: Biographies.
Classification: LCC ML410.D276 B76 2024 (print) |
    LCC ML410.D276 (ebook) | DDC 780.92 [B]—dc23/
    eng/20240125
LC record available at https://lccn.loc.gov/2024003637
LC ebook record available at https://lccn.loc.gov/
    2024003638

for Jim and Greta

CONTENTS

PREFACE

WILLIAM L. DAWSON USED THE WORD "Negro" with pride in reference to himself and others of his race, and thus it appears in these pages, in quotations and in titles such as *Negro Folk Symphony*. I employ the terms "Black" and "African American," both of which are widely and respectfully used in the United States today. I capitalize both Black and White as racial terms. Capitalization of the former is currently a common practice in both academic and journalistic writing, while the latter is less common. I am persuaded by historian Nell Irvin Painter: "We should capitalize 'White' to situate 'Whiteness' within the American ideology of race, within which 'Black,' but not 'White,' has been hypervisible as a group identity."[1]

Dawson almost never referred to the songs at the heart of his musical life as "spirituals," preferring instead "religious folk songs of the American Negro." He believed that calling them something other than "folk songs" obscured that they are part of the nation's folk song heritage. His opposition calls attention to how, by cordoning off folk songs created in the United States by Black people, the term "spiritual" has assisted the category "American folk song" in remaining implicitly White. Out of respect for Dawson's preference, I generally avoid using "spiritual" as a noun in this volume, instead referring to African American or Black American religious folk songs (or, as a shorthand in some contexts, "the folk songs").

In academic writing about music, it is conventional to put the titles of long works in italics (*Carmen*) and those of brief works or component parts in quotation marks ("St. Louis Blues"). This practice can at times be clarifying but subtly ascribes greater weight and significance to longer works and multimovement genres. Conforming to this practice would orthographically bifurcate Dawson's main compositional output into a single major piece, the *Negro Folk Symphony*, and a number of implicitly less-significant choral works such as "There Is a Balm in Gilead." Such an approach would belie the monumental importance of Dawson's compositions for choir. It would also reinforce the racism and sexism that underpin American music scholarship's habitual valuation of music associated with professional musicians and elite, male- and White-dominated institutions above music associated with students and amateurs, and with the spaces and institutions in which women and musicians of color have flourished. In this volume I use italics for all music titles, thereby affording folk songs and choral arrangements the same orthographic respect as symphonies.

Dawson asserted, often in the context of efforts to preserve his copyrights against infringement, that his arrangements of folk songs were works of originality, creativity, and artistry. Accordingly, in this volume I often refer to his labor on arrangements as composition. Neither Dawson nor I would claim that any arrangement, however artistic and original, represents an improvement over the folk song brought into being by his enslaved ancestors.

American culture has changed rapidly over the course of the decade I have spent writing this book, including seismic shifts in the nation's racial consciousness. As a White musicologist whose formal education took place mostly at the end of the twentieth century, I have had much to learn and unlearn in the course of my research and writing on William L. Dawson. I owe a special debt to scholars of color and to the upcoming generation of music scholars, whose critical sensitivity to language has challenged and inspired me. The choices in this volume reflect my current understanding and my best effort to write justly and with awareness. I hope that this work will prove useful even to readers, present and future, whose understanding differs from my own.

ACKNOWLEDGMENTS

MY DEEP GRATITUDE GOES TO University of Illinois Press Director Laurie Matheson, whose steadfast support for this project has been indispensable.

I have been blessed in my dealings with my subject's heirs. Both Milton Randolph Jr. and his daughter Jennifer Randolph have been exceedingly generous and kind.

I owe much to the many dedicated professionals in libraries and archives who made my work possible, including Randall Burkett, Dana Chandler, Rachel Detzler, Cheryl Ferguson, Gary Galván, Lori Ricigliano, Elizabeth Russey Roke, Stuart Serio, Kathy Shoemaker, Frank Villella, and Angela Weaver. Thanks to Philip Tutor for sharing his expertise on Anniston history.

Several people who knew Dawson personally, or had close connections to him, kindly shared their knowledge with me: Wayne Barr, Leslie Burrs, Mark Butler, John Haberlen, James Kinchen, William Krasilovsky, Jennifer Randolph, Bruce Saylor, and Judge Otis D. Wright II. No one was more integral to this project, nor more generous with his insight, knowledge, and warm support, than Dr. Eugene Thamon Simpson, who knew Dawson well; I wish I could share this book with him.

The University of Puget Sound supported this book in many ways, from research funding to sabbaticals to flexibility in course content and pedagogy. I especially appreciate the personal support of President Isiaah Crawford. Thanks to the many colleagues who helped and encouraged me along the way, including Kris Bartanen, Tim Beyer, Geoffrey Block, Julie Christoph, Erin Colbert-White, Kim Davenport, Tracy Doyle, Regina Duthely, Amy Fisher, Yoonseon Han, Duane Hulbert, Rob Hutchinson, Tina Huynh, Emily Johnson, Pat Krueger, Alistair MacRae, Gerard Morris, Nicole Mulhausen, Ameera Nimjee, Dawn Padula, Maria

Sampen, Tanya Stambuk, Jennifer Utrata, Keith Ward, Anna Wittstruck, Jinshil Yi, and Steven Zopfi.

Wonderful students offered insights, asked great questions, and cheered me on over the years, including Eli Chenevert, Sam Crosby-Schmidt, Chris East, Andrew Friedman, Riley Granger, Rhiannon Guevin, Jennifer Kullby, Miguel Ledezma, Dan Levy, Kyle Long, Aric MacDavid, Austin Mangle, Kerry Miller, Ava Price, Rosie Rogers, Jillian Shelver, Drew Shipman, Jules Tan, Robert Wrigley, and countless others.

My heartfelt thanks to the many musicians and scholars who shared expertise and friendly encouragement: the members of the EMRG group, Vilde Aaslid, James Abbington, Dwight Andrews, Houston Baker Jr., Ryan Bañagale, Rebecca Barrett-Fox (and the AGT Monthly Writing Challenge), James Blachly, Karen Bryan, Mark Burford, Marquese Carter, Marva Griffin Carter, Roderick Cox, Minnita Daniel-Cox, Samantha Ege, Arthur Fagen, Matt Franke, Marques L. A. Garrett, Sarah Gerk, Angel Gil-Ordóñez, Sara Haefeli, A. Kori Hill, Ellie Hisama, Joseph Horowitz, Albert R. Lee, Heidi Lee, Katherine Leo, Nathan Link, Anne Lundy, Horace Maxile, Matthew Morrison, Rachel Mundy, Kay Norton, Nathalie op de Beeck, Jason Posnock, Laura Moore Pruett, Eric Saylor, Doug Shadle, Wayne Shirley, Ayana Smith, Jean Snyder, John Spilker, Larry Starr, Travis Stimeling, Darryl Taylor, Louise Toppin, Kristen Turner, Denise Von Glahn, Joe Williams, Josephine Wright, and Trudi Vorp Wright. I am particularly indebted to Naomi André, Sandy Graham, and Tammy Kernodle for their inspiring scholarship and nourishing friendship.

I am forever grateful to my family and friends for their love, patience, and more than a decade's worth of real or well-feigned interest in this project. Jim and Greta, my dear ones, thank you for your excellent company on the long journey. Every page of this book is for you.

WILLIAM L. DAWSON

Introduction

For too long, Black Americans have been taught that success is defined by gaining entry to and succeeding in historically white institutions. I have done that, and now I am honored and grateful to join the long legacy of Black Americans who have defined success by working to build up their own.

—Nikole Hannah-Jones, on her decision to accept a tenured faculty position at Howard University instead of the University of North Carolina at Chapel Hill, July 6, 2021.[1]

ON A WARM ALABAMA NIGHT IN April 2015, an energized crowd filled Tuskegee University's Logan Hall gymnasium, occupying row after row of metal folding chairs. Large groups of Black college students in black concert attire moved purposefully along the sides and back of the room. The Tuskegee University Concert Band sat in front of the stage, instruments gleaming. Behind the onstage risers was hung a crimson and gold banner heralding "The Annual William Levi Dawson Institute for Classical and Folk Music."

Over the course of two and a half hours, amidst interpolations from various speakers and selections from the Concert Band, five choirs from four historically Black universities (HBCUs) performed: Claflin University, Florida A&M University, Alabama State University, and Tuskegee University. Every choir's set featured arrangements of Black religious folk songs (commonly known as spirituals), always beginning with one by William L. Dawson. The almost entirely Black audience responded enthusiastically to every speech and performance, cheering and applauding when soloists hit high notes or otherwise exhibited their skill.

The event was obviously the result of herculean organizational effort, particularly on the part of Tuskegee's Director of Choral Activities, Dr. Wayne A. Barr, and Mr. Warren L. Duncan, Head of the Music Department and Director of Bands. Part of Tuskegee's annual Founder's Day Weekend events, the concert honoring William L. Dawson powerfully demonstrates the pride Tuskegee University takes in this illustrious musical alumnus and faculty member. Also among the weekend's traditional events is the William Levi Dawson Lecture, given each year by a different invited guest on an African American music topic. In 2015 the speaker was Dr. Horace J. Maxile Jr. of Baylor University, who spoke on the incorporation of Black religious folk songs into instrumental works by African American composers.[2]

Central to the story this volume tells is a relationship between a man and an institution. Tuskegee Institute shaped William L. Dawson in profound ways during the years he spent there as a prodigiously talented and ambitious young student. It showed him the power of his potential, endowed him with an enduring self-discipline, and gave him a solid foundation of knowledge and skill that served him well as he went on to acquire music degrees and to launch his remarkable career in music. His Tuskegee education formed the bedrock of his lifelong race pride, his commitment to the well-being of other Black people, and his endless intellectual curiosity about both African and African American history and culture. He took to heart the admonition of Tuskegee's famed first president, Booker T. Washington, to overcome the obstacles erected by racism through hard work and an unfailing commitment to personal excellence.

When Dawson returned to Tuskegee as a faculty member nine years after his 1921 commencement, he discovered aspects of his beloved Institute that he had not perceived as a student: the limited resources, the resistance to change, the power struggles inside the institution, and the political and economic pressures from outside. Nonetheless, many of Dawson's most impressive accomplishments took place during his time on the Tuskegee faculty. The Institute may not have fulfilled his every expectation, but for many years it supported (and was distinguished by) his ambitious choral program, compositional activity, and pedagogy. It was no small blessing that as a faculty member at an HBCU, Dawson did not have to waste his time and energy advocating for the importance of educating Black students, nor for the value of African American music and culture.

Just as Tuskegee Institute shaped Dawson's life, Tuskegee University (as it has been known since 1985) today is marked by his presence. He looms large in the university archives, where his name can be found in school *Bulletins* from 1914–15 to 1955–56, in documents showing the inner workings of the institution, and in countless newspaper clippings attesting to the activities of the Tuskegee Choir under his leadership. A campus lane is named for him, and his grave is located just a few hundred yards from the Tuskegee University Chapel. His music continues to resound on campus, whether from the Chapel, Logan Hall, or a CD purchased at the University Bookstore. He is on the lips of campus tour guides, on the mind of every Tuskegee choral director who has followed in his footsteps, and in the hearts of alumni who still remember singing under his uncompromising leadership.

William L. Dawson is a towering figure not only at Tuskegee, but in the field of American choral music. His arrangements of the religious folk songs of enslaved Black people—people from whom he was only a single generation removed—combine reverence for the songs and their creators with rare artistry and pedagogical insight. Dawson was not the first to arrange these folk songs, but his works are the foundation of this choral genre as it now exists. His approach to Black religious folk songs deeply influenced generations of choral composers and directors; the widely performed choral arrangements of Moses Hogan, Rosephanye Powell, Stacey V. Gibbs, and others can scarcely be imagined without Dawson as predecessor. It is not an exaggeration to say that no one deserves more credit for the fact that these uniquely American folk songs are still widely sung and celebrated today.

Why, then, is his name so little known outside the choral music field? Why is Dawson not among the American composers discussed in music history textbooks alongside his contemporaries Aaron Copland, George Gershwin, and Ruth Crawford Seeger? Why was he the last of the three Black symphonic composers of his generation to have a scholarly monograph written about him?[3]

The present volume offers various answers to these questions. Racism is an unmistakable factor in Dawson's neglect. Others include his relatively small compositional output, the prominence of arrangements in that output, the lower cultural prestige of choral music compared to other musical genres, and the fact that most of Dawson's works were composed for students to perform. Less obvious, perhaps, is the significance of geographical and institutional prestige to a composer's visibility and renown. Aside from a few brief, electrifying moments in the spotlight of major East Coast cities—New York City (Radio City Music Hall, Carnegie Hall, television broadcasts), Philadelphia (Philadelphia Orchestra, the Academy of Music), and Washington, D.C. (the White House, Constitution Hall)—Dawson's life and career were rooted at Tuskegee Institute and in his home state of Alabama.

More than a decade ago, when I was at the beginning of my archival research on William L. Dawson, I constructed a narrative in my mind. Its protagonist was ultimately a tragic figure, a genius whose masterpiece, the *Negro Folk Symphony*, achieved instant acclaim upon its 1934 premiere conducted by Leopold Stokowski. Quickly forgotten by the racist and fickle classical music industry, Dawson spent the rest of his career confined to the choral rehearsal room, arranging folk songs, crushed by the demands of his position at Tuskegee Institute. Because

4

he was Black, he was robbed of his rightful role as the American Gustav Mahler, conducting the New York Philharmonic and producing eight or nine more symphonies. Traces of this narrative appear in my 2012 article, "Whatever Happened to William Dawson's *Negro Folk Symphony?*"[4]

It is fortunate that this volume has taken a decade to complete, for over time I have come to reject most of that narrative. His career at Tuskegee Institute was not a fallback plan. The *Negro Folk Symphony*, a miraculous and brilliant work, is not the crowning achievement of his career. And although anti-Black racism and his response to it unquestionably shaped his professional trajectory, his achievements are nonetheless so numerous and significant that I have come to appreciate how profoundly unjust it is to perseverate on what a similarly gifted White musician might hypothetically have achieved. Dawson was both ambitious and intentional, an artist and educator who made considered decisions about how and where to direct his gifts, and whose legacy is rendered no less momentous by the indifference of the White musical elite.

In celebrating the work of a classical musician whose career was affected by racism, sexism, or other forms of bigotry, it is easy to fall into the trap of lamenting historical discrimination while continuing to uphold discriminatory values. It is not coincidental that the activities out of which so many African American musicians have built their careers—teaching, making music in church, playing gigs, arranging—are not those most respected by scholars of classical music (nor critics, conductors, or arts administrators).[5] The activity accorded the most prestige, the composition of large-scale orchestral works that receive professional performances, requires resources that have until recently been accessible almost exclusively to White (and male) composers: secure faculty positions, institutional support, fellowships and awards, commissions, and the patronage of wealthy White music lovers. If scholars pay disproportionate attention to the Black composers who have composed symphonies, we will wildly misrepresent the history of African Americans in classical music. And in our studies of Black composers of symphonies, it is critically important not to treat that achievement as the only one that really matters, casting every other activity as a paltry substitute for the additional symphonies they might have created in some parallel universe free of racism.

As Nikole Hannah-Jones reminds us, it is all too easy to view "gaining entry to and succeeding in historically white institutions" as the only kind of success that matters. She, like Dawson, chose not to play that rigged and self-abnegating game, instead "join[ing] the long legacy of Black Americans who have defined success by working to build up their own." This volume celebrates Dawson's tremendous success according to this definition.

I | Early Life

AT AGE THIRTEEN, WILLIAM LEVI DAWSON ran away from home to attend Tuskegee Normal and Industrial Institute. Few written accounts of his life omit this dramatic event that launched his education and career. His daring escape points to essential aspects of his character: courage, ambition, and a thirst for knowledge. It powerfully represents his rejection of the grinding poverty, endless physical labor, and routine injustices that his parents, like so many African Americans in the early-twentieth-century South, endured. It helps to paint a picture of William Dawson as a heroic individual whose musical and intellectual gifts lighted his path to greatness.

All of this is accurate, but also incomplete and potentially misleading. Dawson's dramatic escape from Anniston, Alabama, did not represent a repudiation of his roots. The achievements for which he is remembered spring from his Black Southern heritage, and from the lessons he absorbed as a child. In making the heart-wrenching decision to steal away, he began a journey not only toward self-realization, but toward a life in which he could put his prodigious gifts to use on behalf of his family, his community, and his race.

An Anniston Childhood

Calhoun County, in northeastern Alabama, encompasses territory inhabited by members of the Muscogee (Creek) and Cherokee Nations. Anniston, the county seat, was originally a private company town. It was founded shortly after the end of the Civil War by the Woodstock Iron Company, whose White owners located the business there to take advantage of the area's rich natural resources. Opening to unaffiliated residents and investors in 1883, Anniston offered jobs in a variety of industries. Among those attracted by the promise of employment was George Dawson of Dougherty County, Georgia, who had been born into slavery in the early 1860s. He found work in Anniston first with an ice company, and then unloading coal cars in the railyard.[1]

In 1896, George Dawson married Eliza Starkey. The 1860 federal census lists Eliza's paternal grandfather as a property-owning "free inhabitant" of Nashville, Tennessee; she and her parents and siblings are categorized as "mulatto" in the 1880 census. Eliza was literate, and she and at least one of her brothers attended college. George and Eliza's marriage endured until his death in 1924, withstanding even the marital crisis brought about in 1913 by their eldest child's escape to Tuskegee.

William Levi Dawson, named after his paternal grandfather William and his father's brother Levi, was born on September 26, 1899.[2] Two brothers and four sisters followed. The family lived in a Black neighborhood on the south side of Anniston. George left home at 4 a.m. each day to begin unloading coal cars for a dollar per day—a significantly higher and more reliable wage than he would have received as a sharecropper in Georgia, but not one that enabled him to support his family comfortably. Eliza, in addition to the labor of maintaining the home and caring for the children, took in washing and ironing for some of Anniston's White families. As a young boy, William picked up customers' dirty laundry in his homemade wagon and returned the cleaned items a few days later. He also shined shoes and used a bicycle to make deliveries for various stores. From an early age, he strove to follow his father's oft-repeated advice: "Stay out of bad company, don't talk back to older people, and help papa take care of the family."[3] This was wise counsel, given by a man whose life experiences had taught him that safety and survival were ambitious enough goals for a Black man to strive for.

George took his son out of school by the third grade so that he could become an apprentice to a shoemaker, Eli Langston. By this time, William had begun to chafe at the deference that Anniston's White residents demanded of its Black ones, including the instruction that he should call White children "miss" and "mister."[4]

He noticed that Langston, when asked his name by White customers, gave only his first initials, "E. L." The shoemaker explained, "A white man always wants to call a Negro by his first name.... I wish to be treated as a man and not as a boy!"[5] William excelled as a shoemaker while daydreaming about other skilled professions he saw men performing: carpentry, brick masonry, railroad engineering. He imagined himself not only helping his family, but "being something."[6]

Music pervaded William's childhood, beginning with the religious folk songs that his mother sang around the house. It gradually became clear that his interest in music was more than a casual one. The boy often stood outside a local church to listen to the singing at prayer meetings.[7] He heard the Fisk Jubilee Singers when they came through Anniston on tour, and whispered excitedly to his mother upon recognizing the songs they performed as being ones he had heard at home and church. He constructed a musical instrument for himself out of a cigar box and devised dances to go along with the rhythms of music he heard. He admired the trombones at the circus and eventually saved enough money to buy a trombone from the Sears Roebuck catalog.

George disapproved of music as a career, believing that musicians spent their time in honky-tonks and saloons, surrounded by the bad company he hoped his son would avoid. His opposition to William even taking up an instrument was alleviated somewhat by the reassurances of S. W. Gresham, an Anniston grocery store proprietor. A respected figure in the Black community, Gresham led the local band, which rehearsed in his grocery store and performed in the annual Emancipation Day parade. George's concerns were also assuaged when a member of Gresham's band loaned William his mellophone to play at home; this instrument, for whatever reason, was more acceptable to George than the trombone. William taught himself to play, seeking out band members when he had questions, and was soon allowed to join the band. Impressed by his talent and determination, Gresham offered him private lessons; unfortunately the grocer passed away unexpectedly soon after.[8]

Gresham had been a bandmaster at Tuskegee Institute, the Black educational institution located roughly 100 miles north of Anniston, and he regaled the band with tales of Tuskegee and of Major N. Clark Smith, who served as Tuskegee's bandmaster from 1900 to 1904 and from 1907 to 1913. In 1911, Smith and the fifty-member Tuskegee Band stopped in Anniston on a tour to promote the Institute. Dawson was deeply impressed by their performance, their fine appearance, and the fact that the band traveled in style in Pullman train cars. He saw Tuskegee as the "black college mecca" when it came to music, and was encouraged when he heard that its president, renowned educator and orator Booker T. Washington, promised that no student would be turned away from Tuskegee for lack of funds.[9]

Removed from school and working full-time from an early age, William watched as other young people left Anniston to attend nearby HBCUs such as Talladega College, Morehouse College, Atlanta University, and Knoxville College. He saw that his peers came back to Anniston changed and longed to share in that experience. Eliza encouraged William's ambition, knowing firsthand that education would expand her gifted son's horizons. Her support helped him to imagine a path beyond George's instruction to "help papa take care of the family." William opened a savings account at the local branch of the Penny Savings Bank, but also began secretly to stow money for running away in a snuffbox that he hid under the house. Disastrously, his playmates discovered the hiding place and made off with his savings. Dismayed by the setback, he began to pay fifty cents a month to N. W. Carmichael, principal of a local school, to continue his education via evening lessons he kept secret from his father.

Eliza's encouragement kept William's Tuskegee dream alive. In September 1913, a few weeks before his fourteenth birthday, he sold his delivery bicycle for six dollars, enough to cover the train fare. On a Sunday afternoon after his father left for Galilee Baptist Church, William arranged for his trunk to be transported to Tuskegee by a friend and then walked a few miles to a train station outside of town, correctly anticipating that George would look for him at the Anniston station upon returning home from church. After boarding at 2 a.m., William hid in the restroom until the train had pulled away from Anniston. His sister Allie Lee later told him that George struck Eliza and locked her out of the house overnight when he discovered her role in William's escape. The following morning, according to autobiographical notes William wrote years later, his mother "went to the back door, broke the lock, and went in. Another war of nerves etc. went on for some time. My father from then on had nothing to say to anyone." One can only imagine the changed family William experienced two years later upon his first visit home.

The Tuskegee Spirit

When he arrived on the Tuskegee campus in 1913, William Dawson's attitude toward "Pa" Booker, as the students privately referred to Booker T. Washington, was pure reverence. The great man, who had journeyed "up from slavery" (as his 1901 autobiography was titled) to become the most famous and respected African American of his age, embodied the transformation that Dawson sought for himself. Tuskegee Normal and Industrial Institute was unique among the historically Black colleges and universities (HBCUs) established after the end of the Civil War for the education of the formerly enslaved, in that it had had a Black president from the beginning. Washington had arrived on "campus" in 1881 only to discover that Alabama's state legislature had approved $2,000 annually for teacher salaries but had not designated land or buildings for the school. His fundraising, relationship-building, logistical work, and leadership took Tuskegee Institute from mere idea to concrete reality. Under his direction, students literally built the campus, even constructing the kiln to fire bricks for the buildings.

Washington, a graduate of Hampton Normal and Agricultural Institute, was the most prominent advocate for what was known as the "Hampton-Tuskegee model" of Black education, which eschewed the liberal arts in favor of vocational training as a means for African Americans to earn a living and demonstrate their fitness for equal citizenship. In public addresses, Washington encouraged Black Southerners to tolerate racial segregation and to work to improve their material rather than political circumstances, a perspective encapsulated in his "Atlanta Compromise" speech of 1895. Although his accommodationist stance has been much criticized, including early on by W. E. B. Du Bois in *The Souls of Black Folk* (1903), Washington's politics were more progressive than one might assume. Even Du Bois wrote, "It would be unjust to Mr. Washington not to acknowledge that in several instances he has opposed movements in the South which were unjust to the Negro; he sent memorials to the Louisiana and Alabama constitutional conventions, he has spoken against lynching, and in other ways has openly or silently set his influence against sinister schemes and unfortunate happenings."[10] Washington quietly contributed large sums to court cases challenging segregation and Black disenfranchisement. In public, however, to preserve Tuskegee Institute and its people in the midst of the Jim Crow South, he strategically performed what Du Bois called "the old attitude of adjustment and submission."[11]

Throughout his life, Dawson viewed Washington as a hero who dedicated himself to the well-being of the Black masses with whom Dawson identified rather than the "Talented Tenth."[12] He marched in the Tuskegee Band behind Washington's coffin in 1915 and always treasured as a keepsake a flower from the funeral.[13] And despite what critics of the Hampton-Tuskegee model decried as its accommodationism and undervaluing of Black intellect, Dawson's Tuskegee education gave him a lasting belief in his own limitless potential and that of his race. In an interview more than half a century later, he noted that the school's faculty had boasted graduates from Harvard, Cornell, and other top universities, including the first Black graduate of the Massachusetts Institute of Technology and the first to receive an advanced degree from the University of Chicago.[14] He recalled that famous African Americans frequently appeared on campus, and that students learned "Negro history every week, not once a year."[15] He was imbued with the "Tuskegee Spirit," which meant both striving for excellence and demonstrating good character. He recalled hearing from classmates, "Dawson, that's not good enough for Tuskegee."

Like other HBCUs at the time, Tuskegee subjected its students to a strict discipline that included daily room inspections, detailed and tightly enforced daily schedules, and exacting codes of personal conduct, particularly for female students. Dawson's first roommates were upperclassmen, Fayette Washington and R. E. Woodruff, who helped him adjust to his new surroundings; among other things, they encouraged him to change his speech habits. Years later Dawson recalled, "The language that I heard at Tuskegee being spoken by teachers and students of the upper classes [that is, older students] as well as by most of the students was of quite a higher caliber than what I had heard from the lips of most of the kids with whom I had played in the streets of Anniston!" The more formal, "proper" English that he learned to speak (and also write) proved useful in many circumstances throughout his life; decades later, he can be heard using it in recorded interviews. He wholeheartedly embraced the ways of Tuskegee as a young person and always regarded the school as having imbued him with habits and skills that served him well throughout his life.

The evening after he arrived at the Institute, Dawson was given a test covering simple arithmetic and basic literacy skills. Based on his performance he was placed in the C Preparatory Class, the most elementary level. The following day he was sent to the registrar to determine what work he would do in exchange for tuition. He expressed excitement at the mention of "civil engineering," believing it to have something to do with trains, and was disappointed to find himself digging up chert, a sedimentary rock used for the sidewalks and streets of campus. He had several other work assignments over the next few years, including farming, food canning, and fence repair, until musical activities supplanted manual labor as his work for the Institute.

Music was part of Dawson's Tuskegee experience from the beginning. It was present at mealtimes and chapel services, where students were encouraged to participate in the singing of African American religious folk songs. As a 1915 *Bulletin* put it, echoing sentiments expressed elsewhere by Washington, "Special attention is given to the 'plantation melodies' which represent an interesting and instructive contribution by American Negroes to musical art. These melodies express better than anything else the spiritual life and moral struggles of the black race in America. In this spirit, they are sung by the choir and the student body."[16] Dawson's lifelong commitment to the religious folk songs as a uniquely valuable Black contribution to American music took root during these years at Tuskegee.

Soon after his arrival on campus, Dawson auditioned on the trombone, which he identified as his principal instrument. He played poorly but was given the chance to improve, which as he later wrote "was all I wanted." He practiced as much as he could, eventually winning a place in the Tuskegee Institute Band. He was soon also placed in the Dining Hall Orchestra, which played every evening at dinnertime, and in the Chapel Orchestra. In the ensembles he gained familiarity with "the nature, sound, and characteristics" of every instrument, knowledge he would later draw upon as a composer. The bandmaster, Captain Frank L. Drye, gave Dawson opportunities to coach other players and even occasionally invited him to conduct rehearsals. Dawson became highly skilled on both trombone and euphonium, and was featured on the latter in performances with Tuskegee ensembles both on and off campus. He studied piano and harmony with Alice Carter Simmons, Washington's niece. The choir director, Jennie Cheatham Lee, allowed him to observe choir rehearsals and in time to join the choir himself.[17] He began composing; his first work, now lost, was called *Tuskegee Cadet March*. Although Tuskegee did not offer a music degree, with the enthusiastic support of the faculty Dawson received a broad and rigorous music education.

Beginning in 1918, Dawson traveled extensively as second tenor in the Tuskegee Singers, a male vocal quintet that toured to raise money and publicity for the Institute. Touring greatly expanded Dawson's horizons; his travel diaries from 1918 to 1921 record the locations of performances occurring almost daily over periods of months, not only in Alabama and neighboring states but along the Eastern seaboard, from New Jersey to Maine.[18] Dawson also played the trombone on tour; a 1920 performance of his own composition, *Forever Thine*, was a favorite with audiences.[19] In 1921 the quintet joined the Redpath Chautauqua Circuit, a program founded in 1874 to bring lectures, concerts, and other edifying entertainments to communities around the United States and Canada. The speakers he met on the circuit included Russell Conwell, the Baptist minister who founded Temple University, and William Jennings Bryan, the politician and orator soon to gain fame for his role in the Scopes Monkey Trial. He benefited as well from the company of his fellow quintet members, including Charles Winter Wood, a Tuskegee faculty member who introduced him to the poetry of Paul Laurence Dunbar. Touring sometimes brought hardships due to racism; White men harassed them at a train station in Massachusetts, and at times the group struggled to secure lodging. Dawson earned $125 monthly on the circuit, $100 of

Figure 1.1. Dawson, ca.
1918. Property of the
author.

which he sent home to his mother. Defying his father's wishes in order to pursue
an education had ultimately enabled him to become his family's primary bread-
winner.

Dawson had enjoyed attending commencement ceremonies in previous years,
but he found himself unable to share in the celebratory mood of his fellow Tuskegee Institute graduates when his own turn came in 1921. It is possible that the
absence of any family members played a role in his melancholy. He writes that
he went to his room and looked up the word "commencement" in the dictionary.
"From that day on, I considered every subsequent milestone as the beginning of
an unending journey to make something of myself."

Starting North

Along with skills, experience, and confidence, Dawson graduated from Tuskegee with access to a professional network of African American educational institutions. He was quickly recruited to build and lead the band program at Kansas Vocational College. The position required his youthful energy as well as musical knowledge, as he located instruments for the program, taught beginning students how to play them, and directed the twenty-piece band.[20]

Although Kansas Vocational College—Kansas Industrial and Educational Institute, at its founding in 1895—was sometimes called "the Western Tuskegee," Dawson's move to Topeka was no minor shift, geographically or culturally. The first of his steps northward in the 1920s, this relocation was a step in the Great Migration, as Dawson joined more than six million other African Americans between World War I and the 1970s in leaving the Deep South. As for countless others, economic opportunity induced Dawson to migrate. The South's Jim Crow segregation and White supremacist violence were also driving factors for many but do not necessarily seem to have been so for Dawson. His experiences on tour had shown him that no region of the United States offered a haven from racism.

His stay in Topeka was brief yet productive. In addition to working at Kansas Vocational College, Dawson took music classes at Washburn College. The school had admitted students regardless of race or gender since its 1865 founding, but school officials hesitated to admit Dawson because Tuskegee did not give academic credit for music, leaving him no official record of his qualification for study. He asked Washburn for an entrance exam and easily passed, gaining admission. His fellow orchestration students were impressed by Dawson's experience with a variety of instruments, and he relished gaining theoretical understanding to complement his hands-on knowledge. He played in the Washburn Orchestra, and in keeping with his long attraction to low-pitched instruments, he took double bass lessons.[21]

Dawson studied composition with Henry V. Stearns, dean of Washburn's School of Music. On one occasion Dawson brought a piece to his lesson, *Romance for Violin*, that began in F major and ended in D-flat. Stearns admonished him that pieces should begin and end in the same key, but a week later he asked Dawson to play the piece for him again. Recognizing this time that the work was successful, Stearns said, "Dawson, hereafter you write whatever you want to write." He invited the young man to his home, where he played for him a recording of

14

Richard Strauss's tone poem *Also sprach Zarathustra*, which ends in two keys—the most harmonically adventurous music Dawson had ever heard. Struck by his student's talent, Stearns urged him to pursue further study with Adolph Weidig, a German-born composer living in Chicago.[22]

In May 1922, Dawson resigned from Kansas Vocational College and moved to Kansas City, Missouri. His plan was to stay just until he had earned enough money to attend the Pat Conway Military Band School at Ithaca Conservatory. He won a euphonium position in Dan Blackburn's Municipal Band, which gave popular summer concerts in Kansas City parks, by sitting in, uninvited, on a rehearsal and improvising impressively during a repeated section of a John Philip Sousa march. Over the course of the summer, Dawson was sometimes featured as a vocalist with the band.[23]

He added to his income by going door to door in Kansas City's Black neighborhoods, selling the sheet music of *Forever Thine*, a song he had written in 1920 for voice and piano (figure 1.2). He had self-published the piece with the help of a loan from his friend Captain Alvin J. Neely, Tuskegee's registrar and a fellow member of the Tuskegee Singers a few years earlier. Dawson informed potential customers that he was trying to earn his way to Ithaca Conservatory, and later recalled that "not one person turned me down."[24]

What he had planned as a brief stay in Kansas City ended up lasting three years. Dawson learned in 1922 that his father was ill and the family was in danger of losing their Anniston home. (George passed away in 1924, and Eliza followed in 1927.) Dawson, who had been supporting his parents and siblings as generously as he could, knew that full-time study at Ithaca Conservatory would limit his income. And so, when former Tuskegee bandleader N. Clark Smith resigned from Lincoln High School and recommended Dawson as his replacement, the young man accepted the offer—much to the delight of the school's principal, who had observed Dawson's work in Topeka and was eager to hire him. Dawson's decision to remain in Kansas City ended his Ithaca dreams. He did not make his way there until sixty years later, when Ithaca College awarded him an honorary doctorate. Dawson's interest in a career as a bandleader did not die immediately, however: he earned a bandmaster diploma in 1923 via correspondence study through the Frederick Neil Innes College of Band Music in Denver, Colorado. That same summer, he took composition lessons from Felix Borowski at Chicago Musical College.

Dawson served as music director at Lincoln High School until 1925, leading the school's band, orchestra, and choirs, and adding classes in music theory

Figure 1.2. Dawson, *Forever Thine*. William Levi Dawson Papers, series 2, box 15, folder 18. Reproduced by permission of the Milton L. Randolph Jr. Estate.

to the curriculum. In addition, he initiated and led instrumental ensembles in eleven elementary schools, work for which his time in Topeka had prepared him well. Dawson quickly became the most prominent music instructor for children of color in Kansas City's segregated schools. He also began to earn notoriety as a choral conductor, beginning in 1923, to direct the forty-member Ebenezer A.M.E. Church Choir. The group gained citywide acclaim, broadcasting repeatedly on local radio stations WDAF and WOQ.[25] Among those who visited the church balcony to hear Dawson's choir was Cecile Nicholson, who in 1935 would become his second wife.[26]

During his years in Kansas City, Dawson lived at the Paseo YMCA, an African American community center. The building was completed in 1914 with funding from Chicago philanthropist Julius Rosenwald, a friend of Booker T. Washington and longtime member of Tuskegee Institute's Board of Trustees. Dawson's fellow lodgers who became lifelong friends included the groundbreaking artist Aaron Douglas, also a teacher at Lincoln High School, and Roy Wilkins, then the

Figure 1.3. Aaron Douglas, portrait of Dawson, 1935. Tuskegee University Archives.

managing editor for Kansas City's Black weekly newspaper *The Call*, who would in 1964 become Executive Director of the NAACP.

In 1925, when the Music Supervisors National Conference (today known as the National Association for Music Education) held its national meeting in Kansas City, Dawson led the Lincoln High School Chorus in a performance for an audience of over 3,000 people at Convention Hall. The students performed his arrangements of *My Lord, What a Mourning* and *King Jesus Is A-Listening*, concluding with R. Nathaniel Dett's *Listen to the Lambs*. It was the first time a Black choir had been invited to perform at the conference. Dawson's arrangements caught the ear of several publishers in attendance, including William Arms Fisher, who had recently turned the famous Largo theme from Antonín Dvořák's *New World Symphony* into the popular commercial spiritual *Goin' Home* (1922).[27] Fisher invited Dawson to his hotel room to discuss publishing opportunities with the Oliver Ditson Company, but the hotel staff's racist disrespect toward Dawson marred the visit, which led nowhere.[28] He had a better experience with the H. T. FitzSimons Company, which published *King Jesus Is A-Listening* that same year, making it his first published folk song arrangement. *My Lord, What a Mourning* and *I Couldn't Hear Nobody Pray* quickly followed in 1926.

Even though he had traded Ithaca for Kansas City, Dawson was determined to continue his education. In 1922, he sought instruction at the Horner Institute of Fine Arts, a school founded in 1914 to train performers for Charles F. Horner's own Redpath Chautauqua Circuit. (This connection may or may not have been significant to Dawson as a circuit veteran; Horner may simply have been the most convenient place to study.) Because he was Black, he was barred from taking classes at Horner, but he sought and received permission to study privately with faculty members. Every afternoon, after the White students had finished class, Dawson would arrive for lessons in composition with Carl Busch and in music theory with Regina C. Hall.[29] He later asserted that the individualized attention he received from Hall and Busch made this a rare case where racial discrimination worked in his favor. As Marcia Citron has written, however, composers who were barred (whether due to race or gender) from "the full breadth of institutional education" missed out on elements such as "group socialization, individual contacts, and exposure to other ideas" that would have enriched their lives and their art.[30]

Hall, whose support Dawson so appreciated that he still hung her picture on the wall of his home decades later, was disgusted by Horner's racist policies. Like Henry Stearns in Topeka, she avidly encouraged Dawson to continue his composition studies in Chicago with Adolph Weidig; he had been her teacher and was the author of the text she used in their lessons, *Harmonic Material and Its Uses* (Chicago: Clayton F. Summy Co., 1923). Dawson did not have as close a relationship with Busch, but they held one another in warm mutual regard: Dawson appreciated his teacher's "sincere, genuine, and unlimited patience," and Busch commended his student's "ambition, industry and talent."[31]

Dawson was awarded the Bachelor of Music in music theory with honors in 1925, becoming the first African American to receive a diploma from the Horner Institute. Roy Wilkins attended the commencement ceremony with Dawson in 1925, and wrote about the experience at length in his autobiography:

> When we arrived at the Atheneum, a young white woman acting as usher met us at the door. She forced a stiff smile. "We have a lovely little balcony for you," she said. . . .
>
> It turned out that the officers of Horner had told [Dawson]—as nicely as they could—that he wouldn't be allowed to graduate with the white students. He was not to worry, they said, since they would give him his degree the next day.
>
> We all considered walking out right then, but stayed only because we wanted to hear Dawson's composition, a piece for violin, cello, and piano titled "Romance." A violinist and a cellist from the Kansas City Symphony Orchestra and a pianist from Horner came onstage, sat down, and began to play. As the melody bewitched the audience, Dawson sat in the balcony watching, his face drawn, following the music from measure to measure and instrument to instrument.
>
> When the musicians finished, the audience broke into applause that swelled, diminished, and rose all over again. The program identified the composer, and the ovation clearly called for a bow, but Dawson had to sit silently in that balcony looking down at the rest of his class—a great sea of white faces. He said nothing.
>
> Then Senator Henry J. Allen of Kansas rose to give the commencement address. In stentorian tones, Senator Allen . . . congratulated Horner on the way it was building character into American manhood and womanhood. He said nothing, of course, about the way Horner had exiled one of its most promising students to a perch among the pigeons simply because he was black.[32]

Wilkins's anger is palpable in his account. Although Dawson mentioned the incident with some frequency in interviews later in life, he portrayed it merely as one of many personal challenges he had overcome. "I wasn't bitter about it," he told a reporter in 1979.[33]

In time, both the Horner Institute and its founder sought to make amends. In 1931, Charles Horner heard the Tuskegee Institute Choir perform under Dawson's direction at the opening of Radio City Music Hall in New York. Afterward, Horner wrote Dawson a letter apologizing for the discrimination he had faced as a student. In 1963 the University of Missouri at Kansas City, which had absorbed the Horner Institute in the intervening years, presented Dawson with a distinguished alumni award.

After his graduation from Horner, Dawson was ready for the next phase of his education and career. He tendered his resignation from Lincoln High School and moved to Chicago. H. O. Cook, Lincoln's principal, sent a telegram pleading with him to reconsider. Dawson responded on September 7, 1925: "It is always my hope that Lincoln High School—imbued with your spirit of altruism and progressiveness—should grow and develop and anything I can do to promote the progress of the institution, I am willing to do, even to my own hindrance." He was quite specific about what that hindrance entailed: "While I have decided to comply with your request and have plans to do so, it will be impossible for me to report before September 15. I am serving as an arranger, and as a critic of new compositions that come in for publication, for the H. T. FitzSimons Publishing Company, which has also accepted several of my compositions." He noted as well that he had "partially accepted a position as the Head of the Department of Theory at the National University of Music, here in Chicago, which in addition to being rather lucrative affords me the opportunity to pursue my studies."[34] The job offer Dawson referred to (but did not ultimately accept) was probably from the Conn National School of Music, formerly known as the Frederick Neil Innes School of Music, from which he had received a bandmaster's diploma in 1923. Out of loyalty to Cook, he returned to Kansas City and resumed work at Lincoln through the end of the 1925 calendar year. During that time, he continued studying composition privately with Carl Busch. By early 1926, he had moved back to Chicago.

"Everything Is Going My Way"

In January 1925 Dawson toyed with the idea of continuing his education at Oberlin Conservatory.[35] It is not clear what changed his mind, but moving to Chicago was in several respects a better choice. A central destination for African Americans during the Great Migration, Chicago was a bustling economic and cultural hub, offering a wealth of professional opportunities for a skilled and versatile musician like Dawson. Chicago allowed him to further his education while continuing to support his mother and siblings far more easily than he could have in a small college town. He again found lodging at a Rosenwald-funded YMCA building, at 3763 S. Wabash Avenue in the Bronzeville neighborhood.

As he had told Principal Cook, in the summer of 1925 Dawson found work with the H. T. FitzSimons music publishing company, vetting submissions and arranging and editing music. He held a similar post with the Gamble Hinged Music Company. In the mid-to-late 1920s he published, with these companies and with the Remick Music Corporation, several African American folk songs in both solo vocal and choral arrangements (discussed in chapter 3). Remick's head arranger, Charles "Doc" Cook, led a successful Black dance band at Paddy Harmon's Dreamland Ballroom, a White dance hall on the city's Near West Side. Cook held a doctorate from Chicago Musical College (hence his nickname), and it is possible that Dawson's academic pedigree made him an especially appealing fit for a band called the "14 Doctors of Syncopation." After hearing him play, Cook hired Dawson to play trombone in the band, joining members who included the early jazz luminaries Johnny St. Cyr on banjo and Jimmie Noone on clarinet. Dawson sometimes also sang and played euphonium and double bass with the band. It is likely that he played on the four sides they recorded for Okeh Records under the name "Cookie's Gingersnaps" in 1926, and on four recorded by "Doc" Cook and His 14 Doctors of Syncopation in 1927 for Columbia (see Discography).[36] After

Figure 1.4. Doc Cook and His 14 Doctors of Syncopation, Chicago, 1927. Photograph by H. A. Hatwell. William Levi Dawson Papers, series 8, box 52, folder 52. Reproduced by permission of the Milton L. Randolph Jr. Estate.

leaving the Dreamland Ballroom in 1927, Cook's band took up residency on the South Side at the White City Amusement Park's Casino Dance Hall. A photo of the band taken there includes Dawson with his trombone, seated in front of the tuba on the right side (figure 1.4).

Perhaps surprisingly, Dawson did not often bring up his membership in a successful Chicago dance band when interviewed in later years. It is possible that he viewed his time in Cook's band simply as a way to pay the bills. He did not openly disparage jazz, but if he did view it as unserious, undignified, or worse, it would not have been an uncommon opinion among educated African Americans of his generation. Another explanation for his reticence lies in a comment he made in 1974: "I have always maintained the conviction that the richness and vitality of the Negro musical heritage need not, should not be limited to jazz and jazz-derived expression."[37] By downplaying his time with Doc Cook's band in favor of his achievements in classical and folk music, he may have sought to avoid fueling the stereotype that every Black musician is a jazz musician at heart.

Beginning in 1926, Dawson attended the American Conservatory of Music and studied composition with Adolph Weidig, whom both Henry Stearns and Regina Hall had urged him to seek out. Born in Hamburg in 1867, Weidig had known Johannes Brahms and studied with the German theorist Hugo Riemann. He joined the Chicago Symphony Orchestra as a violinist shortly after his 1892 arrival in the United States and became a member of the American Conservatory faculty in 1893, teaching theory and composition. The groundbreaking modernist composer Ruth Crawford studied with Weidig at the same time as Dawson, but there seems to be no record of any interaction between the two students. Weidig was notorious for giving withering criticism, but as Crawford's biographer Judith Tick writes, "because his tactlessness was in part related to his extremely high and uncompromising standards, and because he would 'go all out' for a person who he thought was talented and hard-working, he was not only tolerated but admired."[38]

Weidig clearly thought highly of Dawson, who in addition to being talented and hard-working, had a relatively conservative, Romantic musical style (quite unlike Crawford's) that Weidig favored. Dawson, in turn, had nothing but praise for his teacher, describing him to Regina Hall in 1934 as having been "like a father to me" and having "tried to put me in touch with everything that was good, noble and uplifting."[39] Dawson never forgot Weidig's frequent admonition, which surely resonated with his "Tuskegee spirit": "Das ist gut, aber du kannst besser machen" (That is good, but you can make it better).[40] Dawson had written chamber music in Kansas City while studying with Carl Busch, but he credited Weidig with having immersed him in that genre, and he composed several chamber works during his Chicago period, although he chose not to publish any of them.[41] Dawson related in a 1986 interview that some (unnamed) faculty members at the American Conservatory discouraged him from composing for large ensembles—presumably due to racist assumptions about his abilities, or about what constituted an appropriate goal for an African American composer.[42] Nevertheless, it was during his studies there that he began to compose his *Negro Folk Symphony* (discussed in chapter 4). In June 1927 Dawson graduated with honors, receiving the Master of Music in composition.

Weidig urged Dawson to audition for the Chicago Civic Orchestra (CCO), the training ensemble conducted by the longtime music director of the Chicago Symphony, Frederick Stock, and assistant conductor Eric DeLamarter.[43] In 1926 Dawson won first chair in the trombone section, later claiming he succeeded by reading alto clef better than the other auditioners: "I couldn't play it, either, but Mr. Frederick Stock liked my attempt."[44] Dawson was the first and only African American in the orchestra, and was treated rudely by many other members. Stock and DeLamarter, however, were friendly, encouraging his efforts to speak German (Stock's native language) and regaling him with stories of famous German composers they had known.[45] The CCO's repertoire was to have a powerful impact on Dawson as a composer. The bulk of his *Negro Folk Symphony* was composed as he performed works by Edvard Grieg, Franz Liszt, Jean Sibelius, Bedřich Smetana, Pyotr Ilyich Tchaikovsky, and other European composers whose thematic material drew on folk music. Membership in the orchestra was among his proudest achievements, and although it probably did not pay a salary, it was perhaps the single biggest disincentive to his eventual departure from Chicago. His skill as a trombonist and rapport with the CCO's conductors likely gave rise to the hope that he might ascend to a seat in the Chicago Symphony Orchestra. (In fact, the CSO did not hire its first African American member, trumpet player Tage Larsen, until July 2002.)

Archival materials unfortunately do not make it easy to get a sense of Dawson's social or professional relationships with other African American classical musicians in Chicago. He intersected with the community of Black women in Chicago's classical music world between the wars, giving composition lessons to Margaret Bonds, and crossing paths with Florence B. Price.[46] Rae Linda Brown writes, "there is no evidence that Dawson and Price spent any social time together in Chicago, but the two composers worked together at the national NANM [National Association of Negro Musicians] conventions, where they often provided leadership in the myriad of workshops that were offered." His active participation in the NANM suggests that he cultivated connections with other Black musicians.[47]

It may have been through the NANM that he met Cornella Derrick Lampton, a pianist, organist, and music teacher originally from Greenville, Mississippi. A member of the NANM and its Chicago branch, the Chicago Music Foundation, she served as music editor for the *Chicago Whip*, a Black newspaper. Like Dawson, she was extraordinarily well educated: she graduated from Oberlin in 1912, and in 1917 became the first graduate of Howard University's Conservatory of Music.[48] Later, she studied piano in Chicago with Percy Grainger, who described her as "one of the most gifted persons I have ever heard," and in New York City with James Friskin as a recipient of three successive Juilliard Foundation Scholarships.[49] She was an accomplished performer who appeared on the North Carolina Central University Lyceum's 1926–27 series along with such musical stars as contralto Marian Anderson, baritone Julius Bledsoe, and violinist

Figure 1.5. Cornella Lampton Dawson. William Levi Dawson Papers, series 8, box 58, folder 20. Reproduced by permission of the Milton L. Randolph Jr. Estate.

Clarence Cameron White.[50] Lampton and Dawson married in 1927, one month before he graduated from the American Conservatory.

In the following year, Dawson studied composition with the Danish composer Thorvald Otterström, who was interested in African American music and had created several settings of the religious folk songs as well as composing *American Negro Suite* (1916). Fervently anti-racist, Otterström believed that the excellence of Dawson's compositions would help to break down anti-Black bigotry, and he supported his student's symphonic ambitions.[51] During this time, Dawson also took courses at Crane Junior College in public speaking, educational psychology, the history of education, English, and German. His study of German may have been connected to the newlyweds' dream of touring Europe and continuing their studies there.

Tragically, Cornella Lampton Dawson passed away on August 9, 1928, due to complications from an appendectomy three months earlier. William Dawson's composition *Out in the Fields* (1929), a deeply expressive vocal piece with piano accompaniment that he continued to program frequently throughout his career, was dedicated to his wife's memory. "What a pianist she was," he said in an interview toward the end of his life, one of the few times he publicly mentioned Cornella.[52]

In the wake of this stunning loss, Dawson stayed busy. In the late 1920s he continued as he had always done, both earning a living and developing his skills in a wide variety of musical pursuits. He edited and arranged music for two publishing companies; he played the trombone in concert halls and dance halls; he studied composition privately with Otterström. He submitted compositions to the Rodman Wanamaker Competition for Black composers and won three awards: for his early song *Jump Back, Honey, Jump Back* and for a now-lost Scherzo for Orchestra in 1930, and for the song *Lovers Plighted* in 1931. Each win came with a cash prize—$150 apiece, in the case of the 1930 awards.[53] In September 1929 he was hired to rehearse and direct the choirs at the Congregational Church of the Good Shepherd on Chicago's South Side, a part-time job with a generous $100 monthly salary.[54]

His star may well have been on the rise as a result of a high-profile event a month before the church hired him. The *Chicago Daily News* sponsored a contest to select bandmasters for the "Century of Progress" World's Fair that was to be held in Chicago in 1933–34. Local 208, the Black chapter of the American Federation of Musicians, selected Dawson as its representative in the competition. On August 27 he conducted a sixty-man band and a mixed chorus of twenty-one singers, both of which he had assembled for the contest, in a substantial program that included classic band fare and light classics such as Robert Browne Hall's *Dunlap Commandery March*, Dvořák and Fisher's *Goin' Home*, and Theodore Moses Tobani's *Gems of Stephen Foster (American Fantasia)*. The choir sang arrangements by Harry T. Burleigh of *Go Down, Moses* and *Deep River*, Dawson's own *King Jesus Is A-Listening*, and *Listen to the Lambs* by R. Nathaniel Dett, and likely sang with the band on *Goin' Home* and *The Star-Spangled Banner*.[55] With this ambitious performance Dawson won the Negro division competition. There is no record of his having returned to Chicago in 1933 or 1934 to conduct at the fair itself, but his selection to compete shows how highly he was respected in the Black musical community.

Dawson's growing prominence and record of achievement attracted job offers from several HBCUs between 1926 and 1929. Letters arrived from administrators at Lincoln University (Missouri), Calhoun Colored School (Alabama), Florida Agricultural and Mechanical College, and Prairie View State Normal and Industrial College (Texas). It is impossible to know how seriously he considered their offers, but they could not provide much financial enticement for Dawson to leave Chicago and return to the South. As Vice-Principal Charles L. Yoder of Calhoun Colored School said of the offered salary, "We are willing to do the best we can. What the 'best' of schools of this type may be, you are probably well aware."[56]

A contributing factor to Dawson's disinclination to return to the South may be hinted at in a certificate dated April 10, 1928, certifying him as a "DEPUTY and REPRESENTATIVE" of the County Court of Cook County, Illinois, with "full power and authority to remain in the said polling place from the time the polls are opened in the morning of said day until the polls are closed," in order to "observe whether or not the election is conducted in accordance with the law." Given the determination of the state of Alabama to disenfranchise its Black citizens—it is unlikely that Dawson's parents ever cast a ballot—it must have been deeply meaningful for him to serve as an election official in Chicago.[57] Returning to the Jim Crow South was no small step. That said, many Black educators who attended college in the North did take that courageous step in those years, believing as Dawson did that education was key to improving Black lives and that they bore a responsibility to help their race.

In the end, only one HBCU could lure Dawson away from his busy and rewarding life in Chicago. Tuskegee Institute had been helmed by Robert Russa Moton since Booker T. Washington's death in 1915, and under his leadership in the 1920s it had expanded its college-level courses and begun to offer the bachelor of arts degree. Moton's vision for Tuskegee included a School of Music to rival Howard University's Conservatory, and in the late 1920s Dawson was the target of a recruiting campaign that culminated in Moton himself coming to Chicago to woo him. Dawson recalled:

> I told Moton, "I don't know: I am playing in an orchestra and everything is going my way." Then Moton said, "Bill, what do you have against a homecoming?" I accepted that, so I told him I would come to Tuskegee around Thanksgiving just to talk. Moton was a great lover of music, and he told me over and over how much he wanted a School of Music. The night I arrived on campus Moton showed me the chapel and introduced me to the soloists. The next day he convinced me of his seriousness in creating a School of Music at Tuskegee. He said, "You can get rid of anybody you want to. Do whatever you want to the program."[58]

Dawson implies that Moton's promise of complete control over the new school and its personnel was a tipping point for his decision. The opportunity for a Black man to exercise, in a conservatory-like setting, the authority to which his ability, education, and experience entitled him would have been almost unimaginable outside of an HBCU. Indeed, Adolph Weidig had wanted Dawson to join the faculty at the American Conservatory, but even Weidig lacked sufficient clout to break through the barrier of institutionalized racism.[59]

Dawson had run away from Anniston in 1913 with nothing but ambition and potential. His Tuskegee education had provided him with the skills, discipline, and confidence he needed to excel in the North, even in spaces that were unwelcoming to him as an African American. In the 1920s he made the most of every educational and professional opportunity, becoming by the decade's end one of Chicago's most impressive Black musicians. Returning to Tuskegee would enable him to repay the institution that had fueled his rise, and to equip his Black students for success in a hostile world as he himself had been equipped. Dawson knew himself to be a world-class musician, worthy and desirous of national acclaim. He was prepared to bring Tuskegee with him into the spotlight.

2 | Tuskegee

IT WAS NO SMALL THING WHEN TUSKEGEE INSTITUTE hired
one of its own graduates to establish a school of music in 1930. Three years earlier, R. Nathaniel Dett had written, "I know of no Negro college or normal school
whose director of music has come up through the institution itself. Directors of
music in Negro schools have all had to be imported."[1] William L. Dawson, who
as a student had elicited from Tuskegee the most rigorous musical training its
faculty could provide, had gone on to exemplary educational and professional
achievements in the following near-decade. The ardor with which Tuskegee's
leadership sought him for the faculty reflects that, barely in his thirties, Dawson
was very nearly peerless in the world of African American music education.

Dett (1882–1943) was his most significant role model in this arena. A graduate of Oberlin Conservatory, he served on the faculty of Hampton Normal and
Agricultural Institute beginning in 1913 and was its music director from 1926
to 1932. The connections between the two HBCUs were very strong: Booker
T. Washington was a Hampton graduate and former faculty member, and many
aspects of Tuskegee were based on Hampton. (Tuskegee's second president, Robert
Russa Moton, was also a Hampton alumnus.) Dawson and Dett first met in 1918
when the older man visited the Tuskegee campus, and their subsequent corre-

spondence developed into a lasting friendship.[2] A composer, pianist, and organist, Dett shared Dawson's passion for the European concert music tradition as well as his commitment to African American religious folk songs. Dett and Dawson both strove to do what they thought best for their students and their institutions while also satisfying themselves artistically. Dawson's career at Tuskegee ultimately would prove more prosperous than Dett's at Hampton. As an alumnus, Dawson's values conflicted less often with those of his institution than did Dett's. Relatedly and perhaps even more important, Tuskegee embraced Black leadership from its very founding; this orientation allowed Dawson to wield authority with relatively little of the administrative second-guessing that bedeviled Dett during his time at Hampton.[3]

Dawson's contemporary and closest peer was John W. Work III (1901–67). Work, too, was a product of the HBCU on whose faculty he came to serve, having received a bachelor of arts degree in history from Fisk University in 1923. Work's connection to Fisk was practically genetic: several family members attended, including his father and his brother Julian, and both parents taught there. Like Dawson, Work pursued extensive additional education, studying at the Institute of Musical Art (today known as The Juilliard School), Columbia University, and Yale University. (After he joined the Fisk faculty in 1927 to lead the Fisk Jubilee Singers upon his mother's passing, much of Work's schooling occurred during the summers and while on leave from Fisk.) Work shared Dawson's deep love of African American religious folk songs, producing many excellent choral arrangements in addition to conducting extensive ethnographic research, and he also composed works outside of the choral genre. The two men were good friends and frequently programmed one another's arrangements with their choirs.[4]

The chief precedent for a school of music at an HBCU prior to Dawson's at Tuskegee was the one created by Lulu Vere Childers (1870–1946) at Howard University. Joining the faculty in 1903, Childers built Howard's music department into a conservatory and then, beginning in 1918, a school of music. Like Dawson, Childers cultivated an environment rich with music-making by students, faculty, and renowned guest artists. Judging from the correspondence in the Emory University archives, Childers and Dawson were acquainted but not close.[5]

Aside from the example and support of these far-flung individuals, Dawson's work to shape a music program and a career at Tuskegee Institute was trailblazing and solitary. While his unpublished autobiographical writings and correspondence offer insight into Dawson's feelings during other periods of his life, his perspective during his years on the Tuskegee faculty is relatively difficult to glean. Friends from Dawson's later years say that he did not reminisce much about his faculty experience. Letters, interviews, and even faculty meeting minutes provide some glimpses, but key questions remain difficult to answer: What did it mean to him to serve at Tuskegee? What factors kept him working there long after his school of music was dissolved? Why did he resign when he did? Whatever the reasons for his decision to teach at his alma mater for a quarter century, the following pages attest to that choice's lasting, positive impact on many lives.

Creating the School of Music

According to Moton's July 1931 report to the Board of Trustees, Dawson was hired "to reorganize all the musical activities of the institution and to establish a School of Music that will provide the opportunity for young Negroes to prepare themselves for a career in music and especially to stimulate the development of Negro music as a distinct contribution to American art."[6] This last phrase echoes the rhetoric of the "New Negro" Renaissance, reflecting that Tuskegee Institute's leadership was exploring a more culturally ambitious agenda in this period than before.

The Institute's 1930–31 Catalogue shows how the Music Department stood when he arrived. Not including Dawson, the music faculty consisted of three teachers of piano and two of voice. Six music courses were offered: three at the 100-level, covering music fundamentals and the biographies and works of Bach, Handel, and Haydn, and three 200-level courses on "the harmonic basis of music, polyphonic elements of music, musical appreciation, [and] history."[7] A year later, thirteen people are listed as faculty of Dawson's School of Music:

Robert R. Moton, *Principal*
William L. Dawson, *Director, Composition, Instrumentation, and Conducting*
Hazel Harrison, *Head of Piano Department*
Abbie Mitchell, *Head of Vocal Department, Voice Culture and Repertoire*
Andrew F. Rosemond, *Head of String Instruments Department, Director of the Orchestra, Violin and Viola*
Elizabeth Terry, *Head of the Public School Music Department, Voice and Theory*
Frank L. Drye, *Head of the Band Instruments Department, Director of the Band, Trumpet*
O. Lexine Howse, *Piano and Theory*
Portia W. Pittman, *Piano*
Catherine Moton, *Piano and Theory*
Ernest R. Bullock, *Clarinet and Saxophone*
Alberta L. Simms, *School Music*
Emily C. Neely, *School Music*[8]

30

Several notable names stand out on this list. Catherine Moton, a young Oberlin Conservatory graduate, was Robert Moton's daughter and would go on to marry Tuskegee's next president, Frederick Douglass Patterson. Portia Washington Pittman was Booker T. Washington's daughter, a concert pianist who had studied extensively in Europe; she had joined the faculty two years before Dawson's return. Frank Drye had led the marching band at Tuskegee since 1915 (with a hiatus from 1917 to 1919), but it was Dawson who drew him formally into the Music School's orbit. Hazel Harrison was a renowned concert artist, the first African American pianist to perform as soloist with a European orchestra; her recital at Tuskegee in 1924 had been attended by 1,500 people and written about effusively in the *New York Age*, a major Black weekly newspaper. Abbie Mitchell, already three decades into a remarkable singing and acting career, was to spend only three years on Tuskegee's faculty before returning to the stage; in 1935 she created the role of Clara in George Gershwin's *Porgy and Bess*. Lexine Howse (later Lexine Weeks) had joined the faculty before Dawson and would serve as interim department director after his resignation in 1955.[9]

The national and even international reputation of so many of Dawson's hires shows that he designed a major hub for African American classical music in the

SCHOOL OF MUSIC FACULTY 1934-35

L. to R.: Alberta Lillian Simms, P. S. Music; Frank L. Drye, Bandmaster and Band Instruments; Portia Washington Pittman, Piano; Catherine Moton Patterson, Piano; Orrin Suthern, Organ, Theory; Florence Cole Talbert, Voice; William L. Dawson, Director of School of Music, Composition, Conducting; Hazel Harrison, Piano; Emily C. Neely, P. S. Music; George D. Rankin, Clarinet and Reeds; Dorothy Suiton Chenault, School Music; Andrew F. Rosemond, Violin, Strings. Di?.

Figure 2.1. Tuskegee School of Music Faculty, 1934–1935. William Levi Dawson Papers, series 8, box 60, folder 4. Reproduced by permission of the Milton L. Randolph Jr. Estate.

South. It also points to his sense of his own prominence and potential: although he had left Chicago, he did not see himself abandoning the high-profile professional trajectory he had initiated there. In the end, although his program at Tuskegee turned out very differently from what he anticipated, Dawson was ultimately successful in establishing and maintaining national visibility both for the Tuskegee Institute Choir and for himself.

Dawson's School of Music provided musical opportunities for students at all levels, including a children's division and a preparatory division for secondary students. Students sufficiently prepared to enter what the Catalogue termed the "conservatory" at Tuskegee could pursue the bachelor of music degree in piano, voice, organ, violin, viola, clarinet, trumpet, euphonium, trombone, saxophone, or composition, or they could elect a General Music Supervisor course or Instrumental Supervisor course leading to a bachelor of school music degree. Performing ensembles consisted of three choirs (Girls' Glee Club, Men's Glee Club, and a 100-member Institute Choir), Senior and Junior Orchestras, and a Concert Band. Although the curriculum featured courses based on European classical tradition (music theory, counterpoint, etc.), Dawson was progressive enough to offer a course in arranging for dance orchestra, a practical skill for a Black musician in the 1930s.

The collegiate music program expected much of students. Starting in the freshman year, all music majors were expected to practice three hours a day. In some areas, such as piano and violin, incoming students were presumed already to have had several years of formal music instruction. This was striking at Tuskegee, an institution founded to instruct African Americans who, like Dawson himself, had had little access to formal education before arriving on campus. The significant shift in expectations was necessary: a robust, conservatory-style School of Music could not function if most of its participants arrived musically illiterate and unfamiliar with European classical tradition. Dawson bridged the gap by offering a "Pre-Music Course." This was described in the 1934–35 *Bulletin* as being of "one to two years" in length, "designed for Freshmen who come to Tuskegee Institute to study music as a major subject but have not a sufficient amount of training in music to warrant their entering the Freshman class in the School of Music."[10]

The training required to gain admission was not the only challenge music students faced: the program's fees were substantial. In 1931–32, the *Bulletin* offered an estimate of $400 in expenses "for a school year of 36 weeks for a full course music student," of which only $50 represented college tuition and $184.50 covered room and board; the rest went toward tuition for lessons, access to practice instruments, a music library fee, and other specifically music-related costs. For most Black families during the Great Depression, $400 would have been a very sizable sum.[11] Moton had ended Tuskegee's mandatory work policy for students, but many students worked on campus to pay or subsidize their fees. The experience of future novelist Ralph Ellison, who in 1933 entered Tuskegee as a trumpet student, shows what life in the School of Music could be like for students who had to work:

> [Ellison] reported to the bakery at 5 a.m. and toiled there until 1 p.m. He cooked, cleaned, and served as a waiter. . . . Working in a trough five feet by three feet—using "our hands, arms, and sometimes elbows (ha ha)"—he made flour bread for the students and corn bread for the teachers. He also helped churn as much as fifteen gallons of ice cream every day. After lunch, he practiced on his trumpet alone and then with the band. Following dinner, which was a dignified affair with tablecloths, napkins, and an adult host and hostess at every table, he practiced some more until bedtime.[12]

This strenuous regime of both musical and manual labor resembled the one that Dawson had embraced during his own student years at Tuskegee. (In Dawson's case, the musical exertions had been voluntary, since Tuskegee's music program was not formalized at that time.) Similarly, the strict discipline that he imposed upon members of the Tuskegee Choir, enabling him to create an ensemble polished enough to rival any European chorus, was grounded in the militaristic discipline he had encountered as a Tuskegee student, which had begun to relax during Moton's presidency. The male students in the choir under Dawson performed in their ROTC uniforms, the females in matching skirts and midi blouses, all standing straight and performing with their bodies held still (see figure 2.2.) Dawson insisted on perfect punctuality and unfailingly rapt attention during choir rehearsals. He did not hesitate to hurl his baton or pieces of chalk at those who displeased him, nor to dismiss a member from the choir for a disciplinary infraction. If someone sang a part incorrectly, Dawson would require that individual to stand and sing it alone until it was correct. "Taskmaster" was a word his students frequently used in their reminiscences about him. Like his Tuskegee classmates who years before had admonished him that halfway efforts were "not good enough for Tuskegee," he held his students to the highest standards. He was also tireless in his efforts to support his students' success. His care for students went well beyond developing their musicianship, reflecting his personal understanding of the obstacles and challenges that many of them faced.[13]

Dawson's pedagogical use of the African American religious folk songs at Tuskegee illuminates his approach to educating his choir, and indeed the philosophy of his School of Music more broadly. Through his arrangements of the folk

Figure 2.2. Dawson and Tuskegee Institute Choir, ca. 1932. Tuskegee University Archives.

songs, discussed in detail in chapter 3, he gave students who were two or more generations removed from slavery a way of engaging positively with their ancestors' experiences, spirituality, and artistry. While honoring the songs' meanings and aesthetics, Dawson's arrangements and his approach as a choral director cultivated elements far removed from the songs' original context: a blended choral sound, carefully controlled dynamics and phrasing, and the conscious deployment of styles and techniques derived from the European choral canon. His pedagogy thus conveyed the compatibility and equal value of African American and European musical traditions, instilling race pride in his students while also helping them to master the skills valued most in the European-dominated world of American classical music.

His dynamic, creative attitude toward the music of enslaved African Americans stands in contrast to the attitudes of Presidents Washington and Moton. Although both men championed the singing of the religious folk songs at Tuskegee, believing that they enhanced the students' spiritual, moral, and cultural well-being, they did not ascribe aesthetic motivation to the songs' creators, nor any particular aesthetic value to the songs themselves. At a large public singing event on Tuskegee's campus in 1931, shortly after Dawson joined the faculty, Moton celebrated the "spontaneous, heartfelt, soul-expressive songs," describing them as "primitive and unadulterated."[14] Washington, too, had used words like "simple" and "child-like" to characterize them.[15] In fact, Tuskegee's vocal director Pedro Tinsley had resigned in 1903: "[Washington] wanted me to make the boys and girls there sing loud. I had a class of over 400 voices, and when they sang plantation melodies it was something fierce, the way they would roll them out. Mr. Washington knows nothing about music."[16] Fortunately the Tuskegee presidents under whom Dawson served—Moton, Patterson, and Luther Foster—greatly appreciated what his choir accomplished for the Institute and did not meddle with his aesthetic approach.

Into the Spotlight

In spring of 1931, Samuel "Roxy" Rothafel and His Gang, popular radio variety show performers, went on an eighty-city tour of the United States. In addition to giving performances, Roxy was searching for acts to participate in the opening of Radio City Music Hall in New York City. President Moton, sensing an opportunity, sent Tuskegee Institute's Secretary G. Lake Imes to meet with Rothafel during the tour's Atlanta stop and persuade him to make a detour. The Institute located enough trucks and cars to transport the entourage of 100 from the train station in Chehaw, some 130 miles away, to Tuskegee. The troupe was brought to the campus chapel, where the Tuskegee Institute Choir sang for them under Dawson's direction. Rothafel exclaimed that the choir was unlike any he had ever heard and immediately expressed his desire that it be included in Radio City's inaugural festivities.[17]

Remarkable as the choir already was, Rothafel urged a tour to prepare the students for their high-profile New York City debut. His financial support enabled the choir and its chaperones to engage a private Pullman train, complete with its own dining and baggage cars, making the tour both financially feasible and physically safe for the young Black musicians. In late spring of 1932 they sang in venues around Alabama and Georgia, drawing large audiences in Birmingham, Atlanta, and elsewhere. The programs were comprised primarily of arrangements of African American religious folk songs, often by Dawson himself, but also included Handel's *Hallelujah Chorus* and Grigory Lvovsky's *Hospodi Pomilui*, the latter sung in the original Russian. Audiences responded enthusiastically to the concerts, usually demanding several encores.[18] Beulah Mitchell Hill, writing for the Black daily newspaper the *Atlanta World*, gushed about the beauty and remarkable dynamic range of the choir's sound and described Dawson's directing in words that would be echoed in many reviews of the Tuskegee Institute Choir over the coming quarter-century: "Absolute control marked the entire performance. These young students followed the maestro's baton as though they were directed by some hypnotic power. Dawson . . . evoked these superb melodies seemingly at will, although the music-wise could easily detect the months of strenuous and gifted training that had gone before."[19]

A few months later, on December 27, the Tuskegee Institute Choir made its New York debut at Radio City Music Hall. The opening night program was vividly described by Cy Caldwell of New York's weekly *The Outlook*:

> It was an amazing hugger-mugger, probably the oddest show that any modern audience has seen. It had grand opera, ballets, choruses, a night club revel, a minstrel show, acrobats, choric dancers, a risley act, Francis Scott Key getting his inspiration for the National Anthem, a comedy step dancer, two fat imitators from radio, De Wolf Hopper, the Tuskegee Choir bathed in steam, and Dr. Rockwell, a comic who discoursed on the human skeleton. . . .
>
> In essence, it was two things: the huge spectacle of old Hippodrome days, and vaudeville, incongruously mixed.[20]

The Tuskegee Institute Choir sang three songs: Dawson's *Ain'-a That Good News*, his *Oh, What a Beautiful City*, composed for the occasion and dedicated to Rothafel, and *Trampin'*, this last probably Edward Boatner's 1931 arrangement. Brooks

Atkinson of the *New York Times* wrote that the choir "sang gloriously until the ingenuity of the stage direction drowned it in clouds of Wagnerian steam."[21]

In addition to their featured slot, the Tuskegee Institute Choir took part in a number listed in the program as *Minstrelsy*, which featured many of the evening's performers and concluded the first night's lineup. It was composed by Julius Hosmer, with vocal arrangement by Erno Rapee; Jim Coombs was responsible for the lyrics. Since the inaugural concert did not conclude until after midnight, the New York critics were at their typewriters long before *Minstrelsy* took the stage, making it difficult to know exactly what this number looked like, but it was doubtless an eye-popping spectacle. Judging by a chorus part (titled *Southern Rhapsodie*) in the Tuskegee Archives, the music was a high-spirited mishmash of songs such as *Dixie* and *The Old Folks at Home* along with minstrelesque nonsense ("Dinah's a lulu / She ain't no hoodoo"). While the lyrics are blessedly free of derogatory terms for African Americans, even in 1932 this material was of dubious appropriateness for a Black college choir. Dawson did not mention *Minstrelsy* in his official reports home to the Tuskegee administration.[22]

The mainstream critics wrote many words, most of them scathing, about Radio City's opening night but made little mention of the Tuskegee Institute Choir's participation. By contrast, reports in the Black press were jubilant about the inclusion of the Tuskegee Institute Choir in such a high-profile event. Floyd J. Calvin wrote in the *Pittsburgh Courier* that "this recognition of the Negro is epochal in many ways. It is the first time that a great theater has selected Negro artists for its premiere and then advertised the fact along with other regular advertising; since this is positively the world's largest theater and Radio City is the most gigantic undertaking in modern times . . . the bringing in of the Negro becomes many times significant." Calvin also noted that "'Roxy' has advertised in the Negro press of Harlem for Negro patronage," a first for a Broadway theater not promoting an all-black production.[23]

It must have been an unforgettable and exhausting eight weeks for the 100 students and seven faculty members from Tuskegee. When they first disembarked from the train at Pennsylvania Station, they were greeted by flashbulbs and questions from the press before being immediately whisked away to rehearsal. The choir sang a total of 125 performances during the six-week Radio City engagement. The New Year's Day concert at Radio City, which was broadcast over the radio, featured a newly commissioned oratorio by Hungarian composer Desidir d'Antalffy, conducted by Leopold Stokowski and performed by the Tuskegee Institute Choir and another choir with a 225-member orchestra.[24] (Even with these multitudes, the performance did not quite live up to the oratorio's title, *Voices of*

Millions.[25]) On January 24, 1933, before taking part in a 10 p.m. performance at Radio City, the choir sang five songs for a dinner party at the home of Franklin D. Roosevelt's mother, whose attendees included President-elect Roosevelt. On January 29, the choir sang for capacity audiences at *three* churches: Riverside Church, New Mother A.M.E. Zion Church, and St. James Presbyterian Church. Early in February, after their Radio City appearances concluded, they gave concerts at Carnegie Hall and the Academy of Music in Philadelphia. Their 125th performance of the trip was at the White House, for President and Mrs. Hoover and twenty of their friends.[26]

Amidst this intense performance schedule, there was time for some sightseeing. The choir (along with Dawson and the accompanying Tuskegee faculty and staff members) attended *Lucia di Lammermoor* at the Metropolitan Opera House, visited the Statue of Liberty, heard the Mills Brothers in concert at the Paramount Theatre, and traveled to the top of the Empire State Building. They attended a service at St. George's Episcopal Church at the invitation of Harry T. Burleigh, who had served as a choir member and vocal soloist there since 1894. St. George's had significant Tuskegee ties: the pastor, Dr. J. P. Anschultz, had been friends with Booker T. Washington, and a church vestryman, William J. Schieffelin, was chairman of the Tuskegee Institute Board of Trustees.

While the choir's six featured minutes on the Radio City program elicited little comment from White music critics, their concerts at Carnegie Hall and the Academy of Music did receive some coverage. The critical consensus is well represented by the reviewer for Philadelphia's *Evening Bulletin*: "The outstanding impression left by a program consisting mainly of Negro music was that of the extraordinary discipline of the large group. Mr. Dawson evidently has the gift of drilling a choir into a nearly perfect mechanical unit. Unfortunately the choir seemed to be very much in the harness at all times in last night's program and the temperament usually a characteristic of Negro music appears well curbed."[27] H. H., writing for the *New York Times*, made a similar complaint, attributing it to Dawson's lack of understanding: "As any one knows who has ever attended a Negro religious revival, or, for that matter, listened to Hall Johnson's choir in its early days, the spiritual is an aching or a lyric cry; a music rising irresistibly out of pain and longing; intensely alive in its emotion, spontaneous and vivid in its projection; a contribution to the folk-literature of the world."[28]

These White critics, disappointed that the Tuskegee students did not enact a religious frenzy onstage, or at least provide the satisfying spectacle of Hall Johnson's excellent professional choir, did not realize that fulfilling White fantasies about Black uninhibitedness was antithetical to Dawson's ethos and aims. Indeed, since the first tour of the Fisk Jubilee Singers in 1871, many choirs representing HBCUs had taken pains to differentiate their performance practice both from actual folk singing and from the caricatures found in blackface minstrel shows.[29] The difference was noted by Irving Weil, the *New York Evening Journal's* uncommonly self-aware critic, who gave Dawson credit for the choir's musical excellence while acknowledging that he would prefer to hear spirituals performed "as we imagine they would be sung if no whites were within earshot."[30]

Strikingly, the review of the Tuskegee Institute Choir at Carnegie Hall in the Black weekly *New York Amsterdam News* did not find it lacking in spirit or authenticity: "Good diction, balance, precision in attacks and that natural spontaneity characteristic of the Negro race were displayed by the choir. It is to be hoped that Mr. Dawson will not make the mistake (as some others have made) of training away from these simple harmonies all the sweetness, vitality, emotion and tonal color." For this reviewer, the threat of a lifeless, inauthentic performance was a concern for the future; the concert under discussion was so compelling as to allow a listener to "sit back comfortably, turn his ear stageward and imagine himself in a great camp meeting down South."[31]

Whether critics approved of the performance's aesthetics or not, there was a broad consensus that William L. Dawson was a force to be reckoned with. Months after he and the Tuskegee Institute Choir had returned to Alabama, *American Business Survey* was still singing Dawson's praises:

> It would be unfair to say that the excellence of this choral organization is due to the genius of one man; yet towering above the singers, training their voices, directing the difficult counter-melodies, selecting suitable music and, frequently, producing his own scores is the figure of the choir's distinguished director, William Levi Dawson. A notable figure in the world of music, Mr. Dawson's distinctive contributions have been in the field of native Negro music, and there is no one to gainsay him the position of prominence....
>
> Mr. Dawson has made a unique contribution to American music. A tremendous ovation greeted the choir's every appearance at the International Music Hall. The Tuskegee Choir, under his direction ranks among the truly great choral organizations of the musical world."[32]

Dawson took tremendous pride in his achievement with the Tuskegee Institute Choir at the opening of Radio City Music Hall. Certainly he never performed for a larger audience, nor in a more highly publicized concert, although the premiere of his *Negro Folk Symphony* less than two years later was perhaps an even greater personal triumph. The two events are connected: it was at Radio City that he met Leopold Stokowski, and Dawson took advantage of the opportunity to promote his work. At the inaugural concert in December 1932, when introducing the Tuskegee Institute Choir, Rothafel announced that Stokowski planned to conduct the premiere of Dawson's symphony.

It seemed at first that the New York trip would boost Dawson's choral publication record. The choir's performances attracted the attention of the G. Schirmer Music Company, one of whose managers contacted Dawson during his stay and encouraged him to submit his music for possible publication. When Dawson actually went to the Schirmer offices, however, he was informed that they were "not in the market" for his work, a response that he understood to be motivated by racism.[33] A year later, a Schirmer representative again urged him to submit his music, but by that time he was self-publishing through his own Tuskegee Music Press, using the steam press available on campus. He would continue to publish and distribute his own works until the 1960s, when he entered into an arrangement with Neil A. Kjos Music Company, which focused on music for education; Kjos treated Dawson and his music with great respect.

The Tuskegee Institute Choir created such a sensation in New York that Rothafel offered to extend their contract by an additional four weeks, but it was time for the students to return to their classes. They arrived back on campus on February 11, 1933, to a heroes' welcome. In his report to the Board of Trustees for 1932–33, President Moton wrote that "during their absence from the school the choir sang to at least half a million people directly, besides a vast radio audience in nation-wide distribution of the news reels. It is impossible to estimate the value of this publicity to the Institute." He further noted that "the choir operated well within its budget for the Radio City engagement and incurred a very modest expense for the additional two weeks' time spent in concert engagements in New York, Philadelphia, and Washington, which latter phase was projected with authority of the Chairman of the Board."[34]

The idea of the choir doing a Rothafel-supported tour of the "British Isles, Continental Europe and Soviet Russia" in 1934 got far enough to merit the creation of a glossy promotional brochure.[35] Despite the claims printed thereon, it is not clear whether President Franklin D. Roosevelt or the U.S. State Department ever actually endorsed or offered financial support to an international tour by the Tuskegee Institute Choir aimed at "promoting international and interracial goodwill." The idea generated enthusiasm among Tuskegee administrators, but Rothafel's health was likely too poor to allow him to follow through in 1934. (He had been hospitalized for a period during the opening weeks of Radio City Music Hall and died of a heart attack in 1936.) In 1935 the idea was still on the table, and impresario Alexander Basy made inquiries in Russia on Tuskegee's behalf as late as February 1935.[36]

Dawson himself may have been less invested in pursuing plans for an international choir tour in 1934 because of the impending premiere of his *Negro Folk Symphony*, which occurred in November. The high profile engagement at Radio City, followed soon after by his symphony's well-received performance by the Philadelphia Orchestra, briefly made Dawson the most prominent African American classical musician in the country. One measure of his notoriety: Carl Van Vechten, a central figure in the Harlem Renaissance, took several photographic portraits of Dawson while he was in New York for the symphony concerts (figure 2.3). Suggesting that he had turned his focus away from Tuskegee Institute during this period, he responded to his choir members' congratulatory telegram after his symphony's premiere with the same form letter he used for nearly everyone who contacted him ("So many messages have come to me about the Negro Folk Symphony as to make it entirely impossible for me to make a direct acknowledgment of each one"), without even a personalized note at the bottom.[37]

Figure 2.3. Dawson portrait, November 21, 1934. William Levi Dawson Papers, series 8, box 51, folder 10. Carl Van Vechten photograph © Van Vechten Trust. Reproduced by permission of the Milton L. Randolph Jr. Estate.

Dawson was not simply distracted from Tuskegee Institute, as shown in his letter to President Moton on February 19, 1935. In it, Dawson tenders his resignation effective March 1, cataloging his frustration with matters of budget, enrollment, and equipment for the School of Music. He complains that the students' singing at chapel services "has fallen to a low level" because "no provision is made by the school for two-thirds of its student body to receive [the] systematic instruction necessary." He describes his repeated, unsuccessful attempts to elicit cooperation from various officers of the Institute. He writes that his unhappiness has rendered him unable to compose, and that "trying to work in such a situation as I am being forced to serve is not only unfair to the school and the students but also disturbingly detrimental to me both physically and mentally."[38] Moton and Tuskegee's Secretary G. Lake Imes, who were both away from campus at the time, each wrote to Dawson urging him to reconsider, with Imes even playing on Dawson's sympathy for the ailing Moton: "It is hardly sporting to take a step of that kind with your chief away from home and sick too. You don't step out from under when a man can't help himself."[39] These pleas were evidently successful.

Another source of turbulence for Dawson in 1935 was his serious long-distance relationship with Cecile DeMae Nicholson.[40] Born in Watonga, Oklahoma, in 1910, she had first met Dawson in Kansas City in the mid-1920s, when she was a student at Sumner High School. She received a bachelor's degree from Howard University, where she was a member of the Delta Sigma Theta sorority, then earned a master's degree from the Kansas State Teachers College, going on to teach home economics at Morris Brown College in Atlanta. In 1935 she and Dawson reconnected, and soon he was driving nearly 300 miles to Atlanta for visits. The courtship hit a rough patch when Cecile revealed that another man was courting her. Dawson sent an anguished letter, likely in early September 1935, in which he wrote, "I'll never love anyone else as I have you. I have never loved so deep." He went on, "Everybody here knows something is wrong with me. . . . If we didn't have the inauguration [of Moton's successor] coming on next month, I really think I'd leave Tuskegee."[41]

He offered to end the relationship, but a few phone calls quickly settled things, and the two were married on September 21, 1935. Their marriage was a happy one, enduring until William passed in 1990. Cecile opened a clothing boutique near Tuskegee Institute, the Petite Bazaar, running it for decades. Her loving support for her husband, and the roots she put down as a successful entrepreneur and involved community member, likely contributed to his remaining on Tuskegee's faculty until 1955.

Disappointment and Determination

Despite President Moton's good intentions, the School of Music that Dawson was brought in to create was an uncomfortable fit for Tuskegee. The difficulty faced by overstretched students like Ralph Ellison was mirrored at the structural level by the unsustainable stretching of finances and infrastructure required to run the School itself. The budgets for various components of the music program came from several different divisions, and its rehearsal rooms, classrooms, faculty offices, and music library holdings were physically dispersed across campus.[42] Although the School of Music got off to a spectacular start with the immediate, high-profile success of the Tuskegee Institute Choir, Dawson's program was tenuously positioned over a trapdoor that depended on the support of Tuskegee's president—support that did not last.

In October 1935, Robert Russa Moton was succeeded as president of Tuskegee Normal and Industrial Institute by Frederick Douglass Patterson, a PhD-holding veterinarian and academic who sought to develop and prioritize initiatives that strategically balanced the institution's foundational pragmatism with new ambition. He oversaw the establishment of programs in veterinary medicine, commercial dietetics, engineering, and civilian and military aviation, this last leading to the creation of the famed Tuskegee Airmen. In 1937 he led the institution to be renamed Tuskegee Institute, as it was known until it became Tuskegee University in 1985. Patterson was also instrumental in the creation of the United Negro College Fund in 1944, which helped to counteract lower philanthropic support for Black education during and after the Second World War.

Although in 1935 Patterson married his predecessor's daughter, faculty member and pianist Catherine Moton, he was no special friend to the School of Music. Tellingly, his autobiography does not mention Tuskegee's music program, its choir, nor William Dawson.[43] Whereas his Annual President's Report for 1935–36 states that the Tuskegee Institute Choir and a student quartet had participated in high-profile performances, including on Montgomery radio, the following year's report contains no mention of music. The writing was on the wall: the Board voted unanimously in 1937 to discontinue the School of Music Dawson had been hired to create. Only six students had completed bachelor of music degrees.

Although it was a heartbreaking development for Dawson and the other music faculty and students, from a financial perspective the School of Music had become an expendable luxury for Tuskegee Institute. Patterson's 1938–39 Report celebrated that the year "closed with the smallest actual deficit on record for our work and . . . a further drastic effort has been made to curtail our program to a point manageable within the reasonably assured income and to permit concentration in fewer fields. In this way it is hoped that the traditional vocational and technical interests of our work may be enhanced with a corresponding effort to meet the newer demands in the areas we have elected to serve."[44] Music was sacrificed in this period of austerity and regrouping despite its proven ability to attract positive national attention to Tuskegee.

Now a department instead of a school, the music program was much diminished. In the 1937–38 *Bulletin*, nine music faculty are listed, of whom only four—Dawson, Drye, Rosemond, and Simms—had been on the School of Music faculty. By the 1940–41 school year, these four comprised the entirety of the music faculty, and in the years up to Dawson's 1955 resignation, the faculty never again numbered more than six. The curricular offerings and programs similarly dwindled; the 1937–38 and 1938–39 *Bulletins* state that "the Department of Music has for its specific purpose the preparation of music teachers. To this end it offers a four-year curriculum leading to the degree of Bachelor of Science in Music Education."[45] The *Bulletins* for the following three school years have no listing at all for the music department's faculty or course offerings. When the department resurfaces in the 1942–43 *Bulletin*, it offers a "Joint-Curriculum leading to the B.S. Degree in another school or department and the diploma in music," because "teachers are frequently expected to conduct bands, choruses and orchestras and sometimes to teach classes in music in addition to their regular classroom duties."[46] Two years later, the 1944–45 *Bulletin* makes no mention of a music diploma. Remarkable musicians continued to attend and receive excellent training at Tuskegee, but the music program ceased to resemble the bold edifice that Dawson had created.

He did not relax his standards just because there were no longer any students majoring in music, and the Tuskegee Institute Choir maintained its high level of excellence and acclaim. Although the choir was open to any student who was interested, the dedication required of members was notoriously intense for an extracurricular activity. Clyde Owen Jackson, who graduated in 1949, recalled that the choir rehearsed six times a week: every weekday evening at 6:00, and before the 11:00 chapel service on Sunday.[47] When a concert or tour was approaching, Dawson would schedule additional mandatory rehearsals that sometimes forced students to miss other classes; as another student put it, "Mr. Dawson must have been in good with the President because nothing was ever said about it."[48]

Among the star music students between 1935 and 1938 was Zenobia Powell Perry, who studied piano with Hazel Harrison and was the rehearsal accompanist for the choir. She traced her beginnings as a composer to Dawson. Biographer Jeannie Gayle Pool writes,

Figure 2.4. Dawson conducting choir, ca. 1940s. William Levi Dawson Papers, series 8, box 52, folder 9. Reproduced by permission of the Milton L. Randolph Jr. Estate.

[Perry] remembered, "Sometimes Mr. Dawson would come in. I would get there before the choir got there and I wanted to see what they were going to practice that day. And sometimes I'd begin doodling [at the piano] and he'd say, 'What was that you were just playing?' I'd say, 'I don't know.' He said, 'Well, give it a name and write it down. I want to see it.'"

Zenobia Perry also worked on some arrangements for the choir. Occasionally she would criticize one of Dawson's arrangements: "'That doesn't sound like you right there. This ought to be so and so.' And he'd say, 'Don't tell me what it oughta be...' and then he'd say, 'Now, what did you say that oughta be?' Sometimes there was a collaboration between us for certain phrases of the songs."[49]

The humor and mutual admiration reflected in Perry's account provide a welcome contrast to the more typical depiction of Dawson by his students as a stern disciplinarian. He was a skilled teacher regardless of a student's level of preparation or ability, able to inspire a Zenobia Powell Perry as well as a novice musician.

Jackson describes Dawson's method for working with a choir whose members might have no prior musical training:

> He taught us how to find one (do) and the key of a work in a major key. . . . He would then have us sing up and down the scale. Then he would point randomly to any pitch within that scale and we sing the correct (numbered) pitch. That is, how we began to sing music at sight. Finally, he would have us turn to any page in the school's hymnal and sing any part (soprano, alto, tenor, bass) at sight. Then he would write (difficult) excerpts from anthems and spirituals we were working on for performance and drill us on those. Finally, he would give us a sight-singing test and we were awarded our letter (an emblem much like the school's football, baseball and track athletes were awarded) to wear on a white sweater. Also, he would give individuals "pop" tests. That is, he would just call on you at any time to sing. I can hear him now: "Jackson, sing your part." Since you never knew when that was coming, it kept us alert and learning.[50]

The high level of musicianship that Dawson developed in his students did not focus narrowly on note-reading and sight-singing. On the contrary, his pedagogy was expansive, going beyond music to include lectures on visual arts and literature, scripture, history, politics, and—as a continuous thread—the significance and equality of the contributions by Black people in every endeavor. While modeling formidable intellectual curiosity, Dawson expected his students to develop and nurture their own. Again, Jackson's recollection is vivid: "[Dawson's] guidance along with the learning of Negro history through learning spirituals, made us not only proud to be black, but also know why we were proud. I will never forget when the Head of the United Nations' Trusteeships Division was assassinated and his deputy, Ralph Bunche, stepped into his role, brought peace to the Holy Land, winning the Nobel Peace Prize, Dawson sent us to the library to do research on Ralph Bunche."[51]

He consistently presented African American music, culture, and history as being not only equal to their White-dominated counterparts, but in conversation with them. This is evident in the repertoire that Tuskegee Institute Choir sang, signaling to choir members and audiences alike that the religious folk songs created by enslaved Black people, while essential, were not the only music that the choir could or should perform. Whether performing at Tuskegee or off campus, Dawson frequently programmed European selections, such as works by Pyotr Ilyich Tchaikovsky (*Hymn to the Trinity*) or Handel (an *a cappella* rendition of the *Hallelujah Chorus* was always well received). He also included less well-known composers, including Selim Palmgren (*Summer Evening*) and Dawson's composition teacher Carl Busch (*O Moonlight Deep and Tender*). He made a point of programming art music by Black composers such as Samuel Coleridge-Taylor, whose *Hiawatha* cantatas Dawson conducted on campus with the Tuskegee Institute Choir and Orchestra in 1936, '37, and '38. Dawson was especially eager to program music by his friend and frequent campus visitor R. Nathaniel Dett, which the choir performed almost as regularly as Dawson's own. Dett's *Listen to the Lambs* was a special favorite, perhaps in part because Dawson was pleased to showcase sacred music by a Black composer that did not include overt stylistic references to African American folk music.[52]

Dawson's dedication to Tuskegee and its choir resulted in a choral program that stayed in the national spotlight for decades. Building on the audience it had reached through its Radio City Music Hall appearances in late 1932 and early 1933, the Tuskegee Institute Choir was heard frequently on radio broadcasts across the country, including a weekly series on NBC that launched in October 1937 and ran through March 1938. These programs featured mostly African American religious folk songs—some, according to the Black weekly *New York Amsterdam News*, "in their simplest musical form, as sung in the churches of the Southern rural districts," but most in arrangements by Dawson, Dett, Coleridge-Taylor, Burleigh, and others.[53] The choir also occasionally performed art music by European and American composers on broadcasts.

Ironically, although the 1937–38 broadcasts were made possible through Birmingham's WAPI, the shows were not broadcast in the South; a WAPI spokesperson claimed without further explanation that they had been "prepared especially for listeners in the North and Northeast."[54] This exclusion led Sally Bell of the Associated Negro Press to urge readers around the United States to send letters and telegrams praising their local stations for carrying the Tuskegee broadcasts, and to NBC headquarters requesting that the programs be made available to "more listeners, especially those of the southland whence Negro spirituals originate."[55] The volume of correspondence, sent not only to radio stations but to President Patterson and to Dawson himself, was characterized by the Black weekly *Philadelphia Tribune* as "an avalanche" of support that reflected "nationwide reception . . . unprecedented for this type of program."[56]

The purpose, politics, and artistic quality of the Tuskegee Institute Choir's work on these NBC broadcasts are revealed on a recording of the first of them, on October 10, 1937.[57] The programs were clearly intended to inspire White philanthropic giving to the Institute. The recorded program begins with commentary from an announcer, President Patterson, and Alabama Governor Bibb Graves; the governor (a former member of the Ku Klux Klan) was a sufficiently controversial figure that the *New York Amsterdam News* wrote, "It is being hoped that Negroes and Northern friends of the school will not react adversely to the series because it is ushered in by Bibb Graves."[58] Booker T. Washington receives much praise; the announcer intones that he was "called the Moses of the Negro race because he delivered thousands of Black men and women from the bondage of ignorance and economic slavery with his practical program of industrial education as preparation for useful living." Patterson reassures listeners that "Tuskegee Institute since its inception has emphasized the importance of distinctive contributions from the Negro people as well as the importance of hewing to the common mold in the fundamentals of organized society." Graves, in turn, praises Tuskegee Institute alumni for consistently avoiding prison and the poorhouse.

Layered beneath and featured amidst this troubling rhetoric that seems to reaffirm the most accommodationist aspects of Washington's "Atlanta Compromise" speech, the 100-voice Tuskegee Institute Choir's performances in this first program are unmistakably superb. Rich, blended sound, dynamic contrasts, sensitive phrasing, and impeccable diction mark this as a first-rate ensemble, one whose refinement and control stands in stark contrast to the more exuberant and sonically heterogeneous style of contemporaneous Black choirs like that of Hall Johnson. Singing artful but relatively straightforward arrangements of well-known religious folk songs such as *Deep River* and *Swing Low, Sweet Chariot*, Dawson's choir skillfully negotiates the task of supporting the narrative about Tuskegee's noble-yet-humble history and purpose, while demonstrating a level of Black artistic excellence that far surpasses "the common mold."

In the years that followed, Dawson's Tuskegee Institute Choir maintained a national profile through broadcasts. It was featured in half-hour Sunday morning radio programs broadcast coast-to-coast from the Tuskegee Chapel on the CBS network in 1945 and the ABC network in 1946. In the 1950s, the choir made its mark on television, going to New York City to appear on Ed Sullivan's *Toast of the Town* and on *The Kate Smith Show* in April 1952, again on Christmas Day 1953 and New Year's Day 1954 on *Coke Time with Eddie Fisher*, and on *Frontiers of Faith* and *The Arthur Godfrey Show* in 1955. The choir was also highly visible in on-campus and regional concerts. In April 1938, it appeared at the opening of the remodeled City Auditorium in Atlanta. In March 1939, the choir performed for dignitaries including President Franklin D. Roosevelt, Governor Frank M. Dixon, and Alabama Senator Joseph Lister Hill on Tuskegee's campus. The annual Easter concert drew a large, appreciative audience; in 1950, the choir was joined by members of the Atlanta Symphony in a program that included works by Antonín Dvořák, Felix Mendelssohn, Handel, and Burleigh.[59]

48

National attention was not always an unmitigated good. The Tuskegee Institute Choir began a concert tour on May 22, 1946, in New York City with a nationwide radio broadcast. The next day, it performed at the unveiling of a bust of Booker T. Washington in the Hall of Fame at New York University. The tour continued in early June with performances in a variety of prestigious venues, including the Academy of Music in Philadelphia and Newark's Mosque Theater. One particular venue brought controversy: Washington, D.C.'s segregated Constitution Hall in Washington, D.C., owned and operated by the Daughters of the American Revolution. The DAR's refusal to allow the famed Black contralto Marian Anderson to perform there in 1939 led to her iconic performance on the steps of the Lincoln Memorial, an event sometimes marked as the start of the Civil Rights Movement. In 1946 the DAR persisted in its "White artists only" policy at Constitution Hall. Because President May Erwin Talmadge was an outspoken supporter of segregated education, however, the organization did not oppose the Tuskegee Institute Choir performing in the hall to benefit the United Negro College Fund.[60]

The Washington committee of the UNCF announced that it would not accept funds raised by the choir's performance at Constitution Hall. Dozens of HBCU presidents joined the committee in urging President Patterson to relocate the concert. In a public statement, Patterson—who had founded the

Figure 2.5. Dawson with D.A.R. members Mrs. Jeoffrey Greyke, Mrs. Charles Carrol Haig, and Mrs. Harold L. Hodgkins, June 4, 1946. ACME. Property of the author.

UNCF only four years earlier—refused, saying that he was "unable to see any real gain to be made, either by the United Negro College Fund or Tuskegee Institute," leading a reporter for the *Pittsburgh Courier* to characterize him as having "fought a one-man battle . . . on the side of segregation."[61] The choir's concert took place as scheduled on June 3. It is impossible to know how Dawson felt about the controversy and whether he would have preferred to relocate the concert, but in a 1979 interview he said that the original selection of Constitution Hall as the tour's Washington venue had been his idea. He also noted that "more than 4,000 people walked through those pickets to hear us sing."[62] A review of the concert described the "capacity audience which was about equally divided between the races" receiving the performance warmly, demanding several encores.[63]

While the Tuskegee Institute Choir quickly achieved and then maintained prominence throughout Dawson's years at Tuskegee, he gradually developed a professional profile as a choral director apart from the Institute as well. In 1939 he conducted the All-State High School Chorus in Tulsa, Oklahoma. In 1948 he conducted North Carolina's annual State High School Music Contest and Festival, hosted by North Carolina College for Negroes (today North Carolina Central University), and the following year he led the Kentucky Negro Educational Association's All-State High School Chorus and College Chorus in Louisville. Despite the "State" or "All-State" labels, because segregation was in full force in these states, each chorus was comprised of Black students.

In early December 1946 he was invited to conduct a chorus of about one hundred New York State School Music Association members—fellow educators, mostly White—in the concert that concluded their annual meeting in Rochester. This was the first time that NYSSMA had convened an educators' chorus; that Dawson was invited to direct it demonstrates his growing stature in the American choral field, as well as marking a deliberately progressive step on the part of the association's leadership. The chorus rehearsed six times before performing an impressive program capped by Dawson's own *Out in the Fields*, sung with orchestral accompaniment. According to a report by Tuskegee Secretary Imes, "At the close of the concert, Mr. Dawson was showered with invitations to cities throughout the state to conduct local choruses in programs of his own choosing."[64] Beginning in 1949, Dawson was invited at least eight times to serve as guest conductor of Schenectady's annual "Music for Unity" festival, leading a choir of some 500 high school and junior high school singers. Although most of his conducting energy was dedicated to the Tuskegee Institute Choir, his guest activities positioned him well for the decades of his career that were to come after 1955.

The Break

In the closing years of Dawson's tenure, no sign of a wavering commitment to Tuskegee Institute portended his impending departure.[65] President Patterson was succeeded by President Luther Foster in 1953. Dawson served on Tuskegee's Educational Council in 1953–54, a period when the student retention rate was declining. In Council meetings, Dawson's response to the worrisome trend was to advocate for higher academic standards for faculty and students alike, and for curtailing student leisure time. Amidst a discussion of the library, which students were using as much for socializing as for study, the meeting minutes record the following: "Mr. Dawson felt we do not mean business. If we did we would say what we wanted and see that it was done."[66]

The scholarly rigor that Dawson hoped Tuskegee would both model for and require of its students stood in opposition to the structural neglect of African American education by the state. In the end-of-year report he submitted on behalf of the Music Department in 1954, Dawson shed some light on music education in Alabama: "The Music Faculty attended a music workshop at Alabama State Teachers College, Montgomery, Alabama, during the Winter quarter. . . . A statement by the State Consultant for music gave us a picture of the great activity now going on in the public schools of the State for white children. We hope that the future will deal kindly with all children of the State."[67] Dawson did not tend to be outspoken on the racial politics of his time, but here he acknowledged the racist educational system that had affected the students he worked with at Tuskegee. The excellence of his choir, in particular, stood as a rebuke to a segregated society whose underinvestment in Black education showed how little it valued Black potential. In his work with Tuskegee's Educational Council, Dawson attempted to inspire in his colleagues the same level of compensatory determination and zeal that he had brought to the music program for more than two decades.

Even as he demonstrated his commitment to the Institute as a whole, Dawson was naturally a special champion of the music program. In that same 1954 report to the Board of Trustees, he captures the remarkable scope of activities carried out by the department, the ambitious vision that he continued to pursue for the development of student musicians, and the broader context within which he was operating. Noting that "for the most part, our students come to us with very little or no previous training in the basic elements of music," he described a newly implemented program that put students in groups to receive piano and voice instruction. Scheduling problems made for a rocky first year, but Dawson believed in "the soundness of the project."

He observed that musical outreach had contributed significantly to Tuskegee Institute's "world-wide reputation" over the years, and enumerated twenty-seven activities undertaken during the 1953–54 school year alone, including recitals, performances in parades, concerts on campus and off, and radio and television broadcasts. He noted that this list did not include "the regular duties of the Choir, and the Band; that is, R.O.T.C. formations, line of March, and Chapel Exercises." Having highlighted the many contributions of the music program to Tuskegee, Dawson expressed "hope that in the near future, the Music building will be renovated and made more cheerful! It is also hoped that the recommendations as regard the Choir Room in the Institute Chapel will [be] given serious consideration."[68]

The last year of Dawson's tenure at Tuskegee included one of his most enduring achievements with the choir. On March 21 and 22, 1955, amidst various radio, television, and live performances in New York City, the Tuskegee Institute Choir recorded twelve Black religious folk song arrangements by Dawson, plus one piece each by Burleigh (*Deep River*, adapted by Ralph L. Baldwin and with additional touches by Dawson), Dett (*Listen to the Lambs*), and John Work III (*Rockin' Jerusalem*). The resulting album released by Westminster Records in 1955 sold well and received good reviews, including a brief mention by Ross Parmenter in the *New York Times*, who wrote that "the recording is first-class and the singing is lovely."[69] A St. Louis critic described the record: "Virility rather than sweetness characterizes the composite quality of the ensemble; but its high precision is reflected in close shading and pliancy as well as in crispness of attacks and releases."[70] Kurt List, music director for Westminster Records, wrote to a friend, "In all of my musical and recording experience . . . I have rarely had the pleasure of working with as capable a man as Mr. Dawson. I do not hesitate to say that I think he is perhaps the finest choral conductor in the country."[71] The album was reissued by MCA in 1992 (see Discography) and can be purchased through the Neil A. Kjos Music Company website. It provides an invaluable snapshot of Dawson's signature style, and of the distinctive and remarkable achievement of the last Tuskegee Institute Choir under his direction.

At the end of the 1954–55 school year, the annual Tuskegee President's Report displayed what had for some time been a jarring dissonance between the music program's lowly status and the national prominence of its choir and director. The section on the music department begins tersely: "Tuskegee Institute emphasizes the avocational aspects of music. We do not offer specialized courses for the training of professional music performers." The tone of the next paragraph is very different: "This has been an active year for the Tuskegee Institute Choir.

The group appeared on the United Negro College Fund Series, ABC Radio; the Arthur Godfrey Show, CBS Television and Radio; Frontiers of Faith, NBC Television; and Coke Time, CBS Television. The most outstanding performance was given at the Metropolitan Opera House in New York City at the Convocation of the United Negro College Fund on March 21."[72]

Amidst these activities, Dawson had also reached a national audience with his essay, "Interpretation of the Religious Folk-Songs of the American Negro." Appearing in the March 1955 issue of *Etude*, a widely read magazine for music teachers, this is the only essay he ever published. It offers unique insight into what Dawson thought, at the midway point of a long career centered on the folk songs, was most important to communicate. He begins by noting that despite the consistent popularity of the songs since the Fisk Jubilee Singers began sharing them with the world in 1871, that popularity has not always been matched by understanding. This has led to arrangements and performances "which ofttimes have obscured [the songs'] inspired beauty and done violence to their inherent reverence."[73]

Perhaps surprisingly, Dawson then turns not to an account of the songs' beauty or reverence, but to providing historical details that illuminate the horrific circumstances in which the songs were created. He argues that an understanding of "the cruelties suffered at the hands of masters and overseers, and the agonies and torment of soul which these cruelties produced" is required if one hopes to fully comprehend the spiritual and aesthetic value of the music created by those who were enslaved. At no point in the essay does Dawson lay special claim to the religious folk songs because of his own racial identity or experience, nor does he suggest that the songs are more or less suitable for any arranger or singer depending on their race. To the contrary, he includes himself with his readers as he writes that "we are [removed] from the times and conditions which gave birth to this music," a nod both to the passage of time and, perhaps, to the early gains of the Civil Rights Era. To overcome this distance, Dawson calls his readers to face the history of chattel slavery in the United States, a system that inscribed horrors into the bodies and memories of millions.

The essay goes on to address two specific aspects of the folk songs. The first is the use of dialect, of which Dawson writes: "It is a mistake to think that the dialect of the Negro is only a crude attempt to pronounce Anglo-Saxon words. Careful examination will reveal that instead, it is an instinctive modification of their harsh and guttural sounds to satisfy his natural preference for soft and euphonious vocables characteristic of his native African speech." The second aspect is rhythm, which when performed correctly will combine "a regular, even tempo with elastic rhythms coming forth in large, flowing waves." Pushing back against racial essentialism, he ascribes the weakness of many performances not to the race of the performers but to the limitations of their material: "One often hears the statement: 'No one sings these songs as Negroes sing them.' This is true only in part, because much that could be put on paper, rhythmically and otherwise, is omitted in the transcription." Dawson traces some of his own understanding to the time he spent in West Africa (addressed in chapter 5). In his discussion of dialect and rhythm, Dawson emphasizes the aesthetic excellence of the religious folk songs without drawing any connection to European-derived aesthetics. Deeply rooted in Africa, the songs are excellent on their own terms, and can be understood and performed well by musicians who are prepared to study and take them seriously.[74]

In closing, Dawson's essay returns to the songs' fundamental meaning: "The religious folk-songs of the American Negro are not to be considered lightly. They express the outlet of suppressed emotions and religious fervor; they are the reflection of a deep spiritual experience. The creators of this unique body of song literature seem to have had the spirit of God in their hearts. If the interpreter gives these songs the consideration and study that they require, both he and the hearer are certain to have a rich spiritual reward."[75] The essay thus offers readers a welcome and a promise, but also issues a challenge, using words so carefully measured that it is possible to overlook their boldness. The religious folk songs of enslaved Black people in the United States, which for generations have widely been sung, transcribed, arranged, reinterpreted, heard, and loved by Americans of every race, demand more than mere affection or admiration. Dawson calls on music teachers to understand that the songs demand a deep intellectual commitment to the history, artistry, and humanity of Black people.

In the same month that his quietly radical essay was published in *Etude*, Dawson tendered his resignation from Tuskegee Institute after twenty-five years of service. There are many plausible reasons why he chose to leave when he did, but it is difficult to pin down a definitive answer or catalyzing event. The *Pittsburgh Courier* attributed the resignation to "alleged dissatisfaction with 'working conditions.'"[76] A letter Dawson wrote to a friend in February 1955 provides some detail: "Since September, none of my experienced tenors were permitted to sing in the Choir because of a foolish ruling instituted in September. Believe it or not, I have had but three (3) freshmen tenors all year. Believe me, it has been a most unhappy experience."[77] According to Mark Hugh Malone, who interviewed Dawson extensively for his 1981 dissertation, he resigned "to devote time to composing and to the ever-increasing requests for leading clinics and workshops."[78] Similarly, the official explanation given by Tuskegee's administration was that he wanted more

54

time for "creative work."[79] One might guess that a salary dispute played a role in the sudden departure; in April 1955, the Board of Trustees expressed concern that low faculty salaries were failing to retain Tuskegee's best teachers.[80] Dawson's friend Eugene Thamon Simpson dismisses the idea that pay was a factor, noting that Dawson's salary was among Tuskegee's highest and pointing out that in any case, he didn't get into teaching for the money. Simpson's theory is that Dawson was fed up with "uncaring administrators that were always trying to . . . please Mr. Charlie to get the necessary funding."[81]

An article in Tuskegee's *Campus Digest* shows that although he tendered his resignation in the spring of 1955, Dawson's absence the following fall came as a surprise to many:

> Returning choir members, faculty and students to commence the Fall term, were shocked as they read the Daily Activity Sheet announcing the resignation of William L. Dawson, Head of the Music Department and Director of the Tuskegee Institute Choir. The general feeling running through the student body suggests a very great loss of a most capable and highly talented person. . . .
>
> In an interview, Mr. Dawson expressed grave consideration concerning his resignation which was submitted last March. His reaction reminded one of a person whose decisive traits have been strained to the breaking point. His attitude was one of a deep devotion, unable to detach itself from something cherished so many years.[82]

The 1955–56 Catalogue still listed Dawson as a faculty member.

The timing of his departure was particularly awkward as 1956 marked the Diamond Jubilee of Tuskegee's founding, and the annual Founder's Day program, held that year on March 25, was even more momentous than usual. Had Dawson remained, music would doubtless have played a major role in the festivities. As it was, the music faculty headed by Lexine Weeks agreed that it was best not to make the program too long.[83] The exercises featured the Tuskegee Institute Choir only once, directed by faculty voice teacher Ethel Hardy Smith. They performed a work by Wolfgang Amadeus Mozart.

The exclusion of Dawson's music was counterintuitive, since during the ceremony Tuskegee Institute awarded him an honorary Doctor of Music degree. The citation in the printed program praises Dawson for "conferr[ing] great distinction not only upon yourself but upon your alma mater as well." It acknowledges that he made the Tuskegee Institute Choir "one of the most widely admired ensembles of our time." Strangely, it spends three times as many words on his career outside of Tuskegee, emphasizing his instrumental compositions, including not only the *Negro Folk Symphony* but also several earlier works (including the lost *Scherzo* and *Break, Break, Break*) that were never published. Meanwhile, his frequently performed choral masterpieces like *Ezekiel Saw de Wheel* and *Ev'ry Time I Feel the Spirit* are swept, unnamed, into the category of "arrangements of Negro spirituals."[84] (As noted in the preface, Dawson rejected the term "spirituals" as misleading and marginalizing.) Dawson recalled this event with little warmth.[85]

In 1989, scholar James G. Spady wrote a tribute to Dawson in which he described his conclusions upon first meeting the man whom "some members of the so-called Tuskegee cognoscente had warned me . . . was very hard to deal with":

> Philosophical, satirical and highly cosmopolitan, I left [Tuskegee] fully convinced that here was a Black artist who represented the very best in the race, the very best in humanity. The fact that so few Tuskegee students or faculty had a precise understanding of the contributions that he had made and continues to make revealed to me just how much strength it takes to walk among the living dead. How much further the institute would have progressed had it afforded its most celebrated son, a Chair in Negro Folk Music, sufficient capital to support various research projects in the U.S.A. and elsewhere?[86]

Spady's anger makes for cathartic reading, but Dawson himself was not prone to bitterness. While it is true that he fought many battles on Tuskegee's faculty, he had remained for a quarter century because he found the battles worth fighting and had won enough of them to persevere. Certainly in the mid-twentieth century, Tuskegee Institute had offered Dawson more administrative and budgetary authority, and more aesthetic autonomy, than he could have expected at any other American institution that might plausibly have hired him. After his resignation, half of his professional life was still to come, bringing many rewards and much satisfaction.

In a different world, Dawson might have become conductor of a major professional orchestra while creating the kind of large-scale works that bring a composer lasting fame and prestige. He was more gifted and skilled than many of his White contemporaries who did enjoy such opportunities. Although his country's racism unquestionably played a role in shaping the course of Dawson's professional life, his decision to spend years of his prime on the faculty of Tuskegee Institute was not a fallback plan, but rather a reflection of his commitment to that institution, and to Black education. His work at Tuskegee was deeply meaningful to him and touched many students' lives. In addition, he served as a powerful role model for generations of Black music educators, particularly those on the faculty of HBCUs. Anyone tempted to lament that Dawson did not have a glorious career as an orchestral composer would do well to consider who benefited most from his career as it played out.

3 | Vocal Music

FROM THE START, WILLIAM DAWSON WAS equally drawn to both vocal and instrumental music. He was entranced as a child by the trombone players at the circus and by the Fisk Jubilee Singers when they performed in Anniston. As a child he sang at home and in church, created his own stringed instrument, and joined the community band on the mellophone. By early adulthood he was a skilled trombonist and euphonium player, and had some proficiency on the double bass; he was also featured as a vocal soloist with the Tuskegee Singers and in Dan Blackburn's Municipal Band. In the 1920s he directed choirs in schools and churches, performed in a symphony orchestra and a dance band, and organized and directed a choir and ensemble that successfully competed at the Chicago World's Fair.

As a composer, too, Dawson's output included a wide range of genres. His first composition was the now-lost *Tuskegee Cadet March* for wind band. The first composition he published was a sentimental love song, *Forever Thine* (figure 1.2). During the 1920s he composed several works that he never published, ranging from solo and chamber pieces to a one-movement work for chorus and orchestra titled *Break, Break, Break*. By the time he joined the Tuskegee faculty in 1930, the two disparate genres in which he would make his most indelible mark were already identified: he had published several choral arrangements of African American religious folk songs and composed his *Negro Folk Symphony*.

Between 1930 and 1955, his compositional output tipped decisively toward choral music. In this period he published thirteen arrangements, most of which remain staples of the American choral repertory to this day. He composed just one additional orchestral work, *Negro Work Song*, discussed in chapter 4. After leaving the Tuskegee faculty his compositional efforts, albeit limited, grew more diverse again: he spent significant time revising his symphony and published seven short choral works in various styles. A list of Dawson's compositions, both published works and those in manuscripts held at Emory University, is provided at the end of this volume.

Dawson's most frequently performed works are his choral pieces based on African American religious folk songs, and up until the recent surge of interest in his *Negro Folk Symphony*, they have also been his best known. That these pieces are canonic repertoire for American high school and college choirs has not translated into widespread fame for Dawson outside of the world of choral educators.[1] Innumerable students in the United States have sung "spirituals" without knowing (or long remembering) who arranged them, and even more Americans have unknowingly heard Dawson's music performed in choir concerts. This speaks largely to the fact that school ensemble directors often (and understandably) spend more rehearsal time rehearsing than they do explaining the background of the music being rehearsed.

Compounding the quasi-anonymity common among composers for school choir is the anonymity of Dawson's source material. The religious folk songs by Black people enslaved in the United States were part of an improvisatory oral tradition. They had no known authors or composers and were in the public domain. Dawson's settings of the songs, and his original works that evoke them, are so sympathetic to the original creations, and to their creators, that it is possible to overlook their artistry—and in so doing, to fail to hear Dawson's compositional voice. This chapter seeks to draw attention to that exceptional voice as it is heard in his vocal music, and particularly in his choral settings of African American religious folk songs, where his influence on the genre has been profound.

Early Arrangements

William Dawson's choral arrangements had many predecessors, from the hymn-like settings performed by the Fisk Jubilee Singers on their historic tours beginning in 1871 to the artful anthems of Harry T. Burleigh and R. Nathaniel Dett. In fitting the folk songs for the concert hall, such arrangements tended to abandon the textural and rhythmic complexity that typified the songs' original, culturally distinctive, communal expression. Beginning in the 1920s, Hall Johnson and Eva Jessye wrote arrangements that strove to capture and preserve the effect of the songs as they had originally been sung. Although both Johnson's and Jessye's professional choirs cultivated a performance style that evoked the timbres and textures of African American communal folk singing, they still sought above all to please audiences. By focusing on the songs' effect on listeners, all of these arrangers fundamentally transformed songs that enslaved people had brought into being not for an audience's pleasure but for their own sustenance. Zora Neale Hurston identified the difference in 1934 when she wrote, "There never has been a presentation of genuine Negro spirituals to any audience anywhere."[2]

William Dawson's pioneering arrangements of the religious folk songs not only balance the aesthetics of African American folk music and European-American concert music, but also honor the original purpose of the songs: to bring life to those who sing them. His works have influenced every subsequent generation of arrangers in the genre while remaining fresh, appealing, and widely performed in their own right. Dawson brought the compositional tools of European art music to his arrangements: principles of harmonization and voice leading, word painting, polyphony, and form. At the same time, his arrangements maintain many of the songs' folk characteristics, including rhythmic complexity, call and response structures, and linguistic creativity, thereby maintaining a strong connection to the songs' origins. Dawson used European compositional techniques not to "elevate" the folk songs into European-style art music, but to make the songs as useful and meaningful for their new singers and settings as they had been for his ancestors in slavery. His hard-earned formal training allowed him to fit the songs to these contexts by magnifying their expressiveness, their effectiveness in performance, and their pedagogical usefulness.

Dawson's first published arrangement, *King Jesus Is A-Listening* (FitzSimons, 1925), already displays several features that mark his unprecedented, influential approach, and decades later he chose to include it on the Tuskegee Institute Choir's 1955 LP.[3] Adhering to the folk song's verse-chorus form, the *a cappella* arrangement begins straightforwardly with the chorus:

Soprano section:	King Jesus is a-listening
Full choir:	All day long
Soprano section:	King Jesus is a-listening
Full choir:	All day long
Soprano section:	King Jesus is a-listening
Full choir:	All day long to hear some sinner pray.

The choir's response to the soprano section's call features the syncopation found in much African American music, while the harmony of this first chorus sticks to the three chords most common in traditional Western European harmony (I, IV, and V). All of this is well-trodden territory for the genre. Dawson's special touch begins to show when the chorus is repeated. At the last choral response, the meter shifts temporarily from two beats per measure to four, and the text is extended by two words (indicated by added italics): "All day long, *my Lord*, to hear some sinner pray." A slowing tempo combines with held notes on "long" and "Lord" to depict the length of the wait. At the final line, "to hear some sinner pray," the harmony becomes more expansive, and the phrase concludes with a plagal (or "amen") cadence that might be expected in a hymn. These compositional choices emphasize the two key themes of the song's text: waiting and prayer.

The final chorus of *King Jesus* provides a satisfying final heightening of these twin themes. The intensity of the waiting is accentuated, as "all day long" is repeated three times with rising pitch and increasing fervor, climaxing on a high, sustained chord sung by the entire choir. Highlighting the theme of prayer, the concluding phrase ("to hear some sinner pray") features the work's most chromatic harmonies, descending expressively to a final reprise of the "amen" cadence. The combination of lugubrious harmony and downward trajectory can be heard as the sinner's tearful return to Jesus through prayer, with the serene final chords implying comfort and forgiveness. Dawson's harmony and rhythm bring the text vividly to life.

The verses of *King Jesus* provide a contrasting texture: while the rest of the choir hums a simple accompaniment, the soprano section or soloist sings the melody. The text features some dialect:

1. The Gospel train is a-coming,
   'tis rumbling thro' the land,
   I hear dem carwheels a-rolling
   Get ready for that train.

2. I know I've been converted,
   I ain't a goin [*sic*] t' make-a no 'larm,
   My soul's been anchored in my Jesus,
   And the devil can't do me no harm.

The inconsistency of the dialect—a single "dem," versus "that" and "the"—reflects the piece's early publication date. Dawson's later choral works tend to be more consistent, using either "th" or "d" throughout an individual arrangement. As a rule, Dawson does not shy away from dialect when it proves rhythmically apt or "euphonious," as he argued in print was the original song creators' goal in their "instinctive modification of [the] harsh and guttural sounds" of English.[4] That Dawson did not use dialect merely to simulate folk authenticity may be inferred from his sparing inclusion of it; a few of his arrangements (such as *Jesus Walked This Lonesome Valley* and *Swing Low, Sweet Chariot*) use only Standard English. It is interesting to note that Georgia Scott, the soloist on the Tuskegee Institute Choir LP, pronounces the first verse's "-ing" words as "in'" ("comin'," "rumblin'," "rollin'"), presumably with Dawson's approval. He was famously meticulous in his notation and insistent upon performers' fidelity to the score, but Scott's pronunciation suggests that Dawson sometimes notated less dialect than was stylistically acceptable to him in performance.

While *King Jesus* and *My Lord, What a Mourning*, another choral arrangement published in 1926, clearly point toward the iconic works of Dawson's Tuskegee years, three other African American folk song arrangements published soon afterward show Dawson exploring a different approach. *Jesus Walked This Lonesome Valley* (Gamble Hinged, 1927), *Talk About a Child That Do Love Jesus* (FitzSimons, 1927), and *You Got to Reap Just What You Sow* (Gamble Hinged, 1928) were published in SATB choral versions and as solo vocal pieces. All feature piano accompaniment, in contrast with the exclusively *a cappella* folk song arrangements that Dawson published thereafter.[5] 1927 was the year of Dawson's tragically brief marriage to pianist Cornella Lampton; the presence of these elegant piano accompaniments may be due to her influence. *Jesus Walked This Lonesome Valley* is poignant and effective, reminiscent of some of Burleigh's songs in the tastefully chromatic harmonic language, the piano's graceful supporting textures, and the dramatic pathos (rare for Dawson) of the piece's climax. *Talk About a Child*, an intimate expression of faith, features beautiful shifting harmonies and smooth, layered textures. Of the three, *You Got to Reap* has the most noteworthy piano part, with flowing parallel chords and atmospheric harmony evocative of music by Claude Debussy. Relatively little known, these early settings deserve to be performed more often.

Tuskegee Triumphs

It would be difficult to overstate how groundbreaking Dawson's iconic Tuskegee-era choral pieces are—and yet they are so popular, and their influence is so pervasive, that it is easy to take them for granted. All of his folk song arrangements reward close analysis; the following pages take up just three examples, chosen from among Dawson's most popular works.

The infectiously tuneful *Ain'-a That Good News* (first published in 1937, revised in 1974) seems straightforward at first. Subtle Dawsonian touches emerge upon closer inspection, beginning with the addition of a syllable to the traditional title, *Ain't That Good News*. It is possible that the added syllable, the first of several such interpolations into the text, was drawn from oral tradition, but it is not found in John W. Work's nearly contemporaneous version. The interpolations give Dawson's melody the syncopated bounce that distinguishes his arrangement.[6]

> I got a crown up in-a the Kingdom,
> Ain'-a that good news!
> I got a crown up in-a the Kingdom,
> Ain'-a that good news!
> I'm a-goin' to lay down this worl',
> Goin'-a shoulder up-uh my cross,
> Goin'-a take it home-a to my Jesus,
> Ain'-a that good news, good news!

The text, in which Dawson employs far more dialect than in *King Jesus*, receives a rhythmic setting that feels so natural as to seem inevitable. It is, in fact, distinctively his own. He copyrighted his *Ain'-a That Good News* and spared no energy or expense in protecting this and his other choral arrangements against infringement by those who assumed that signature elements of his pieces were simply parts of a folk song in the public domain. At least two infringing arrangements tellingly titled *Ain'-a That Good News* were taken off the market as a result of Dawson's vigilance.[7]

Several aspects of *Ain'-a That Good News* highlight the distance between the original folk song and Dawson's creative and sophisticated work of art. The harmony in particular offers subtle delights along the way. In general, the tonal center is clear, dissonance is kept to a minimum, and the harmony is triadic and straightforward. The first exception comes toward the end of the first chorus, at the words "Goin'-a take it home-a to my Jesus." The 3rd scale degree is unexpectedly harmonized by a major seventh chord in which the melody note is the seventh (IV^{M7}). The effect is both tender and fleeting, perhaps suggesting a moment of intimacy with Jesus amidst the otherwise extroverted piece. In the last verse ("I got a Saviour in-a the Kingdom"), the chords grow increasingly more colorful as they lead to a long, climactic dominant ninth chord (G^9). By never resolving in a functional way (to C major, or V), this chord makes the phrase "Ain'-a that good news" sound more like a question here than it does at any other moment in the piece (although it is never punctuated with a question mark). The final phrase returns to the most solid and basic triads, answering stoutly with the chords of an "amen" cadence: "Good news, good news, my Lawd, a-ain'-a that good news!"

Dawson's compositional imagination and craft are on display in the variety of vividly expressive textures featured in the verses. In one ("I got a robe up in-a the Kingdom, / Ain'-a that good news!"), the sections of the choir overlap as they eagerly enter, one after the other. In the next verse ("I got a Saviour in-a the Kingdom"), the section singing the melody is accompanied by quiet, fervent, rhythmic agreement in the other voices ("good news! good news!"). And in a verse that Dawson added in his 1974 revision ("I got a harp up in-a the Kingdom"), a thinned-out texture is joined to a suddenly slower tempo and the expressive marking "with restrained joy." The shifts of texture hold the listener's interest; more importantly, they provide challenges for the singers and make space in rehearsal for considering and interpreting the text of each verse.

This interpolation of a new verse in an established classic is in keeping with Dawson's characteristic perfectionism and ongoing creative engagement with his completed works. He may also have sought to make the arrangement more infringement-proof by enhancing its compositional distinctiveness. The added verse is controversial among choral directors. Eugene Thamon Simpson, for instance, writes, "I have always held that the original and shorter version is a perfect creation that accurately reflects the text. The revision, which completely interrupts the excitement and animated flow of the work is, in my opinion, a mistaken version, to me, totally incomprehensible. I . . . told [Dawson] that I liked the original better and have performed only it."[8] On the St. Olaf Choir's 1997 CD, *The Spirituals of William L. Dawson*, conductor Anton Armstrong includes the new verse but disregards the section's slower tempo marking. Choir director James Kinchen's very first thought upon meeting Dawson for the first time in 1979 was to ask his hero why he had revised *Ain'-a That Good News*. Dawson explained that the new verse attempts to capture the quiet intensity of a Black congregation continuing to sing while the deacon prays—an explanation that Kinchen found persuasive.[9]

On the other end of the affective spectrum from *Ain'-a That Good News* is Dawson's *There Is a Balm in Gilead*, first published in 1939. This piece flows so serenely as to disguise the skill and imagination with which the composer distributes the melody and harmony among the four sections of the choir and the soloist. At the start of the piece, the tenor section sings the melody, accompanied by the sopranos humming a gentle and almost completely static note above, and by the altos who softly sing a nearby countermelody. By keeping the upper three voices quite close to each other, in a comfortable range for each and with only the mildest of dissonances between the parts, Dawson creates a marvelously peaceful atmosphere in the first statement of the chorus:

> There is a Balm in Gilead, to make the wounded whole,
> There is a Balm in Gilead, to heal the sin-sick soul.

The last word is elided with the entrance of the bass section beginning a second iteration of the chorus. This entrance expands the piece's pitch range downward, and the upper voices respond with overlapping echoes of the first four words—first the sopranos and altos, then the tenors—as if the basses' entrance has created ripples on the previously placid surface of the music. After a moment of polyphony, the four sections join together in the unified chordal movement most typical of a four-part hymn setting. Because the first several measures of the piece have presented such a variety of textures, the conventional hymn texture takes on expressive significance when it arrives: as they sing together for the first time, the four sections present a culmination, a "making whole." Throughout the arrangement, the texture coalesces each time the chorus returns to the topic of healing.

Another subtle but noteworthy aspect of Dawson's *There Is a Balm* lies in his use of meter changes to shape the phrases. A look at earlier versions of the song in collections by Dett and Work makes clear how original Dawson's approach was. Work sets the melody in 2/4 time throughout. Dett does as well, adding a fermata to extend both "whole" and "soul."[10] Dawson's arrangement, marked "Slowly," largely stays in 4/4 time, which implies a slower and more flowing approach; significantly, he shifts the meter to 6/4 for the measure that includes the word "whole," thus attaining a similar effect to Dett's fermata but with more precision as to how long the note should be held. The meter shift brings two additional benefits. First, he almost always sets the word "whole" to two slurred half notes or a whole note, a clever touch of madrigalism. Second, the distinctive meter shift marks the arrangement as Dawson's, which helped him identify many infringing versions over the years. (To this day, many hymnals contain undeniably Dawsonian *Balm*s.)

There Is a Balm in Gilead offers singers the satisfaction of singing with great expressiveness, and also the technical challenge of singing long phrases at a slow tempo. In the performance on the Tuskegee Institute Choir LP, Dawson's direction emphasizes these qualities. Taking a tempo even slower than marked, the choir and tenor soloist Otis D. Wright balance perfectly between intense control and heartfelt expression, demonstrating remarkable breath support and keen attention to Dawson's direction. One can hear the warm care that Dawson extended to his students in the way the choir swells to support Wright (then a Tuskegee alumnus) as he sings the verses. It is a lovely, poignant performance.

If Dawson has a choral masterpiece, it may well be *Ezekiel Saw de Wheel* (1942), a work that he fought almost literally to the death to protect against infringement (as chapter 5 will detail). Again in this work we see the composer's commitment to the Black folk origins of the song coupled with a generous helping of effective, technically challenging compositional elements drawn from European tradition, all in service of giving a highly rewarding rehearsal and performance experience to young singers. The depth, specificity, and brilliance of *Ezekiel*'s references to both African American and European musical traditions make it stand out even among Dawson's other folk song arrangements.

The most immediately distinctive element of *Ezekiel Saw de Wheel* is its fascinating text:

> Ezekiel saw de wheel,
> 'Way up in de mid'l of de air. . . .
> De big wheel run by faith,
> De lit'l' wheel run by de grace of God

Before considering the content of these words, note the dialect, which Dawson again uses deliberately to elicit the desired sounds and rhythms. At the piece's brisk tempo, a choir would struggle to enunciate "The little wheel ran by the grace of God" without a loss of rhythmic precision.

The kaleidoscopic vision of a wheel turning in a wheel is captured throughout the arrangement by recurring polyphonic textures, but most spectacularly in a section near the end of the piece. In this passage, the alto, tenor, and bass sections are each split into two or more parts that gradually build a dizzying texture of overlapping, very short patterns repeated many times: "doom-a-loom-a," "wheel in a," or simply "wheel." Once the texture is fully established and buzzing along, the sopranos enter (also divided into two parts) and sing the refrain melody several times. This intensely repetitive and harmonically static section brilliantly captures the sense of awe and suspended time that a divine vision might bring. Additionally, it evokes a repetitive, trance-inducing spiritual practice of singing and moving in a circle, rooted in Africa and enacted during slavery, known as the ring shout. Dawson may well have been the first to evoke this practice in a composition.

Alongside these gestures that embrace the culture handed down to him from his enslaved ancestors, Dawson incorporates in *Ezekiel* an exceedingly subtle allusion to one of the most famous works of European choral music. The last verse of the song features this text:

> Some go to church for to sing an' shout
> Before six months dey's all turn'd out

Unusually for Dawson, he adds text to the original folk song's lyrics: a series of "hallelujahs" between these two lines that evoke a congregation's unrestrained exultation. However, the texture (in which the three upper voice parts respond to the bass line in homorhythmic chords) and insistently repeating rhythmic motive (short-short-long) call to mind the texture and motoric quality found in much late-Baroque music. This, coupled with a shift from B-flat major to D major that lasts only for the five measures of interpolated "hallelujahs," marks an unmistakable but easily overlooked nod to the *Hallelujah Chorus* from George Frideric Handel's *Messiah*, also in D major.

The fact that Dawson smuggled *Hallelujah* into an evocation of Black congregational exuberance stands as a particularly brilliant instance of Signifyin(g). This concept, theorized by Henry Louis Gates Jr. in the context of Black literary studies, is helpfully defined by Samuel A. Floyd Jr. for music: "Musical Signifyin(g) is troping: the transformation of preexisting musical material by trifling with it, teasing it, or censuring it. Musical Signifyin(g) is the rhetorical use of preexisting material as a means of demonstrating respect for or poking fun at a musical style, process, or practice through parody, pastiche, implication, indirection, humor, tone play or word play, the illusion of speech or narration, or other troping mechanisms."[11] Dawson was careful not to make the allusion obvious, which would have created a comic effect, something that he never sought to do in any of his religious folk song settings. As he wrote in his *Etude* article of 1955, "It cannot be stressed too strongly that these songs should never be sung for the expressed purpose of amusing or even entertaining the hearer."[12] Dawson's Handel reference is a brilliant inside joke to be enjoyed in the rehearsal room, but one not made at the expense of the folk song's dignity. To the contrary, the allusion draws a pointed parallel between musical expressions created across the Atlantic from one another and afforded very different levels of cultural prestige.

Dawson wrote wonderful choral music before and after his time on the Tuskegee faculty, but perhaps it is not coincidental that the pieces he created for his beloved students are the ones that seem most indelible in the repertoire. The urgency and care with which he crafted music to educate, encourage, and fortify his singers is palpable in these works.

Early and Late Rarities

In 1961, almost two decades after *Ezekiel Saw de Wheel*, Dawson published *In His Care-O*, an arrangement of the spiritual *I Am in His Care* (also known as *Jesus Got His Arms Around Me*). Although the later arrangement is distinctive in many ways, it recalls *Ezekiel* by incorporating the vocables "doom-a loom-a" in a repeating section that disrupts the work's forward momentum. The repetition lasts only a couple of measures in the later work, creating a disorienting moment rather than a whole tableau. While less obviously connected to text painting than in *Ezekiel* ("a wheel in a wheel"), the repetition in *In His Care-O* could be said to depict immersion in God's love, present in the text "Jesus got His arms all-a around me."

In a rehearsal of *In His Care-O* in the early 1980s, Dawson urged the Ithaca College Choral Union to "feel like you are giving yourself a hug for happiness as you are singing this song."[13] The text conveys a comforting, intimate relationship with God:

> One day as I was a-walkin'
> Down de lonesome road
> Well de spirit spoke unto me
> An' it filled my heart with joy!

Unlike *Ezekiel*, whose text emphasizes spiritual dangers ("Your foot might slip an' yer soul get lost") and examples of what not to do ("Some go to church fo' to sing an' shout"), Dawson's text for *In His Care-O* focuses on the joy of closeness to God:

> Oh, well, Daniel, he was a good man, Lord
> He prayed three times a day
> Well, de angels hist their windows,
> Just to hear what Daniel had to say.

The piece's rhythmic bounciness and uplifting text are reminiscent of Dawson's earlier works *Ain'-a That Good News* and *Ev'ry Time I Feel the Spirit*. Unlike those earlier works, however, a good deal of *In His Care-O* is devoid of syncopation. For example, the opening lines suggest the speaker's plodding movement "down de lonesome road" with a suitably pedestrian, on-the-beat rhythm. The first touch of rhythmic vitality comes at the first threefold statement of "care-o," but the word is set to an on-the-beat "Scotch snap" (short-long) rhythm, not a syncopated one. Syncopation finally makes an appearance in measure 17, where the bass section (in parentheses below) starts to offer energetic, accented commentary on the main text:

> (Now, le' me tell you now)
> Once I'm in His care, (Hallelujah, Lord)
> A-in-a my Saviour's care, (Now, le' me tell you now)
> Once I'm in His care, (Sing it over, Lord)
> A-in-a my Saviour's care

The main text, too, begins to include some off-beat accents at the words "in His care."

The trend toward greater rhythmic unpredictability and energy continues in the remainder of the chorus:

> Oh, Jesus got His arms all-a around me
> No evil thoughts can-a a-harm me
> For I am in his ka-ō, ka-ō, ka-ō.

By spelling "care-o" as "ka-ō," Dawson allows the singers to pronounce the word very quickly and emphatically while avoiding the Italianate flipped "r" that "care-o" might elicit. The interpolation of extra syllables ("all-a," "can-a a-harm") unleashes a new level of rhythmic energy. The most intriguing thing about this passage is that it deviates not only from predominantly on-the-beat rhythms but also from the predictable 4-measure phrase structure of the preceding measures. Starting at "Oh, Jesus," very few words are articulated on the downbeat of the measure, leading the listener to hear an asymmetrical meter even though the notated meter never deviates from four beats per measure. The rhythm and accents create the following structure:

(6 beats)	Jesus got his arms all-a a-
(3)	round me no
(5)	evil thoughts can-a a-
(3)	harm me for
(4 + 4)	I am in his
(4)	ka-ō, ka-ō,
(held)	ka-ō.

The section's syncopation and metric dislocation is layered over an unflagging beat, creating an overall effect that seems to invite body movement from singers and listeners alike. The harmony compounds the invitation by settling briefly into stasis (again echoing *Ezekiel*), the basses staying on the tonic note while other sections embellish the main chord by dipping down a half step and back up again—a technique reminiscent not so much of folk music as of close harmony singing by popular groups such as the Mills Brothers. At the "doom-a loom-a" moment later in the piece, the bass line traces a veritable boogie-woogie pattern, furthering the connection to popular music.

All in all, *In His Care-O* is a remarkable departure from Dawson's earlier folk song arrangements, both in its stylistic affinity with popular music and in the inclusion of elements likely to evoke smiles and even delighted laughter from the audience, including the boogie-woogie bass line, the sudden shift to a faster tempo

68

for the last three pages, and the exclamation ("ho!") that concludes the work. With this original piece, Dawson celebrated a variety of African American musical traditions while letting go of some of the weight that history and situational necessity brought to his arrangements of folk songs for the Tuskegee Institute Choir. It is also tempting to connect the work's statement of joyful confidence in God's protection to its composition at the height of the Civil Rights Movement, when many African Americans and their allies were courageously "walkin' down de lonesome road" toward racial justice.

In the decades of his career that came after his resignation from Tuskegee, Dawson's commitment to spreading knowledge about African American religious folk songs and other Black contributions to American music culture continued unabated. As chapter 5 will discuss, his target audience expanded significantly in this period to include Black and non-Black choral singers and fellow educators across the United States and beyond. He came to take particular pleasure in working with several collegiate male glee clubs, whose repertoire and spirit was considerably lighter than his usual fare. He developed an especially close relationship with Bruce Montgomery and the University of Pennsylvania Glee Club. In his memoir, Montgomery wrote about the surprise twenty-fifth anniversary celebration that the Glee Club arranged for its leader in 1981:

> Perhaps the most astonishing surprise of all was the appearance of the Glee Club to sing a song by William L. Dawson. I learned later that the club had written to Dawson months before asking his price to commission a new work for the occasion. He had written back, I'm told, refusing the commission. But, he added, he would write the work for love! Unknown to me, he had sent the music ahead and then come up to Philadelphia days before the event at his own expense. Greg Suss came in from New York to rehearse the new music each midnight. Then Bill secretly rehearsed the club in the piece and, on my big night, there he was in the ballroom to conduct the premiere performance of "Dorabella." I make no apologies for the fact that as I hugged dear Bill after the surprise performance, I wept freely from joy and love.[14]

Dorabella is an interesting work that is seldom performed and has not been professionally recorded, although the TTBB score is available from Neil A. Kjos Music Company. Its text, written by Dawson, is short and silly:

> Before I married Dorabella I was her pumpkin pie,
> Her precious peach, her honey lamb, the apple of her eye.
> But after years of wedded life, this thought I pause to utter:
> "I find I'm none of these things, I'm just her bread and butter."

The musical setting, by contrast, is complex and fascinating. It evokes a simple Anglo-American folk song but deviates from simplicity with surprising shifts of rhythm, meter, tempo, dynamic level, tonality, and harmony. *Dorabella* showcases Dawson's flair for counterpoint, coupling the trivial text at one point with an amusingly high-flown quasi-fugue. The piece's technical demands are a testament to the first-rate skill of Montgomery's glee club. It is not surprising that a piece simultaneously so silly and so challenging has not become a choral staple; nonetheless, it succeeds brilliantly as an homage to Montgomery and his group.

A peculiar sort of companion piece to *Dorabella* is *The Rugged Yank*, another example of Dawson's work outside of the African American folk idiom. Originally titled *The Mongrel Yank*, he first published it in 1930 with Gamble Hinged Music Company; in 1971 he revised and retitled the work, publishing it with Kjos. Like *Dorabella*, with which it shares a key (B-flat major), humorous secular text, abrupt contrasts, and technical difficulty, *The Rugged Yank* gives the impression of having been composed for fun, and Dawson programmed it regularly in his later work with glee clubs. The text by Allen Quade is wild-eyed patriotic doggerel, including lines like the following:

> In the roar and gore of battle I'm a swearin', tearin' Yank!
> When I hear machine guns rattle, cuttin' down our chargin' rank,
> I'm a fightin', fightin', bitin', blightin' rugged [originally "mongrel"] Yank!

These lyrics receive from Dawson a vivid and none-too-serious musical setting. It can be heard as a satirical treatment of bellicose American masculinity: the music, evocative at times of a sea shanty, is bombastic, dissonant and harmonically restless, heavily accented, and wildly energetic. Dawson's inclusion of two quotations of the song *Hail, Columbia!* (labeled as such in the revised publication) highlights a stylistic similarity between the song and some of Charles Ives's more rambunctious and accessible songs, such as *The Circus Band* and *Charlie Rutlage*. Although I have not encountered evidence that Dawson was familiar with music by Ives, it is conceivable that *The Rugged Yank* was inspired by the older composer. Ives's collection, *113 Songs*, was published in 1922, and Dawson studied with several composers in the 1920s who could have exposed him to it. Conjecture aside, the style, mood, and lyrical content of *The Rugged Yank* mark a startling departure from the music for which Dawson is best known.

Two other early works further expand our understanding of his compositional range. *Break, Break, Break* is a setting of an Alfred Tennyson poem that concludes:

> And the stately ships go on
> To their haven under the hill;
> But O for the touch of a vanish'd hand,
> And the sound of a voice that is still!

> Break, break, break
> At the foot of thy crags, O Sea!
> But the tender grace of a day that is dead
> Will never come back to me.

The manuscript dates from the mid-to-late 1920s. The poem's subject matter raises the possibility that Dawson conceived the piece after the death of his first wife, Cornella Lampton Dawson, in 1927. The William Levi Dawson Papers include a version of the piece for chorus and piano, and one for chorus and orchestra. A third manuscript promises an arrangement for chorus, piano, and organ, but the organ part is left mostly blank.

Break, Break, Break is highly dramatic, harmonically chromatic but tonal, and draws upon a variety of textures, tempos, and rhythms to set the different stanzas of the poem. Dawson was sufficiently satisfied with the composition to secure a readthrough by the Chicago Civic Orchestra when he was a member in the late 1920s, despite the hostility of many of the organization's White players toward its lone Black musician.[15] For whatever reason, Dawson never published the piece, nor did he program it at Tuskegee or afterward.

Another piece from this same period is *Out in the Fields*, dedicated "in memory of my beloved wife, Cornella." It was first published by Remick Music Corporation in 1929 and remains available today through Neil A. Kjos Music Company. Dawson published versions for solo voice and for chorus, both with piano accompaniment; he also created, but did not publish, arrangements for orchestra and for wind ensemble. Unlike *Break*, this piece was an enduring favorite of Dawson's, and he programmed it with some regularity throughout his career. It sets a poem by the White American poet Louise Imogen Guiney (1861–1920):

> The little cares that fretted me,
> I lost them yesterday,
> Among the fields above the sea,
> Among the winds at play,
> Among the lowing of the herds,
> The rustling of the trees,
> Among the singing of the birds
> The humming of the bees.
>
> The foolish fears of what might happen
> I cast them all away
> Among the clover-scented grass

Among the new-mown hay,
Among the husking of the corn
Where drowsy poppies nod,
Where ill thoughts die and good are born,
Out in the fields with God.

Dawson's harmonic language in this piece is consonant, lush, and warmly expressive, very much in a late-Romantic idiom. There are numerous instances of the tasteful word-painting he employs in his folk song arrangements, such as the hypnotically swaying melody at "drowsy poppies nod," and he employs an enjoyable variety of textures in the setting for choir. The piano supports the fairly taxing vocal parts while also playing a significant, independent role in the piece's overall effect. *Out in the Fields* does not evoke any African American musical styles, but the sincerity and artistic care with which Dawson sets this religious poem are entirely characteristic of his output.

If he had created only his three or four best choral arrangements, William Dawson would have left a monumental contribution to the corpus of American music. The layers of knowledge, understanding, skill, creativity, and commitment that he combined in those works are profound, and unique to him. Of course they were not his only creations, even in the category of vocal music. And entirely outside of that realm, Dawson composed one very different piece that now appears poised, at last, to win him the recognition that he has long deserved.

4 | Instrumental Music

WILLIAM L. DAWSON COMPOSED SEVERAL INSTRUMENTAL pieces, one of which is by far the most significant in every respect, including its importance to him. Some others are discussed briefly at the close of the chapter, and all are listed at the end of this volume.

The *Negro Folk Symphony* presents a marked contrast to the choral music that otherwise dominates Dawson's catalog. To state the obvious, the symphony is a long, multi-movement orchestral work. Its generic precursors and contemporaries, performers and performance settings, and likely audiences are worlds apart from those of pieces like *Ain'-a That Good News*. And whereas Dawson arranged more than two dozen folk songs, he composed only a single symphony. The *Negro Folk Symphony* may appear to be an incongruous creation next to his canonic works for choir.

Considered in light of Dawson's biography, however, the symphony does not appear at all anomalous. His intellectual ambition, which led him to run away from home at an early age, fueled the extensive education that equipped him to compose in a variety of genres. His passion for music was always equally divided between instrumental music and vocal, and between the African American and European traditions that the *Negro Folk Symphony* brings together so powerfully.

Like his indelible choral works, his symphony was a labor of love that stretched across decades.

Both Dawson's three-minute folk song arrangements and his three-movement symphony confront the legacy of slavery in the United States. Each, by drawing on and preserving the religious folk songs, lifts up his Black ancestors' spirituality and creativity, implicitly condemning the dehumanizing treatment they endured. His choral works, by appropriating elements from European choral tradition, allowed Dawson to expose students to classical music and its techniques without reifying the boundary between Black folk music and so-called "high art." His symphony is more direct in its confrontation of the nation's unresolved past, specifically depicting the violence and anguish of the slavery experience and even musically enacting a symbolic repair of the broken link between Africa and her descendants in the New World.

The Early History of the *Negro Folk Symphony*

A news article at the time of the work's premiere reports that it "represents four years of work, which was interrupted by the death of [Dawson's] wife [Cornella] . . . a year before its completion."[1] If this account is accurate, then he began composing the symphony around 1925 and completed the first version in 1929. In 1932, when the Tuskegee Institute Choir performed at Radio City Music Hall, Dawson made the acquaintance of Leopold Stokowski, famed conductor of the Philadelphia Orchestra. Less than two years later, in November 1934, Stokowski conducted the first performances of the *Negro Folk Symphony*.

Two other African American composers' symphonies had received premieres not long before: William Grant Still's *Afro-American Symphony* in 1931, with Howard Hanson conducting the Rochester Philharmonic, and Florence B. Price's *Symphony in E Minor* in 1933, performed by the Chicago Symphony under Frederick Stock. These debuts may have inspired Stokowski to program a work by an African American composer for the first time. Dawson's Alabama roots may have compounded his symphony's appeal to Stokowski, who was deeply concerned about the Scottsboro Boys case and had written to the Governor of Alabama on behalf of the nine Black boys and men falsely accused of rape.[2] Doubtless the most important factor in Stokowski's decision was his enthusiasm about the *Negro Folk Symphony* itself; he would hardly have programmed the work otherwise.

The actual concert dates were determined shortly beforehand. Dawson later recalled: "While I was attending a football game with Captain Frank Drye in

Savannah, Georgia, I received a telegram from Stokowski to send the score and the parts to the Symphony immediately. I went to Chicago and got the parts from Frederick Stock. He pleaded with me, 'We will play it on Thursday.' I replied, 'No, Mr. Stock, I must take it to Philadelphia.'"[3] It is striking that Stock, whom Dawson knew from having played trombone in the Chicago Civic Orchestra, apparently intended to perform the *Negro Folk Symphony* in 1934—presumably with the Civic Orchestra rather than the Chicago Symphony, given Dawson's immediate willingness to forego the promised performance. Dawson did not provide a date for these events, but it was not much later when, on November 1, Stokowski sent a telegram informing Dawson that the Philadelphia Orchestra had begun rehearsing the symphony, expressing his excitement, and requesting programmatic titles for the symphony, originally called simply *Symphony No. 1*, and its individual movements.[4]

Dawson immediately provided not only the requested titles but a full program, making explicit the symphony's racially specific concept. It is not clear why he initially offered only a generic title; he may initially have believed that it would garner more performances, or be taken more seriously.[5] Contradictorily, years later he said that the title *Negro Folk Symphony* was inspired by his distress when a commentator at a concert in 1933 failed to mention that Antonín Dvořák's *New World Symphony* was inspired by African American folk songs. Dawson said that he promised himself in that moment, "I'm going to title [mine] *Negro Folk Symphony*. Can't remove that title."[6] (As will be discussed below, in recent years it has turned out that one can, in fact, remove it.)

The first performance of the *Negro Folk Symphony* occurred just two weeks after Stokowski's telegram. Despite the compressed timeline, Dawson was able to attend several rehearsals. In a 1971 interview, he described being unhappy upon first hearing the piece played and brooding over the thought of having put so much time and money into a symphony that was doomed to fail. After the first rehearsal, Stokowski offered the despairing composer a shot of vodka and reassured him that the musicians simply didn't know the piece well yet. A few rehearsals later, everyone was full of optimism, and members of the Philadelphia Orchestra told Dawson that they loved his symphony.[7]

On November 14, 1934, the *Negro Folk Symphony* had its premiere at the Academy of Music in Philadelphia. Dawson's piece closed the first half of a Young People's Concert that also included various unnamed Eastern European dances, Maurice Ravel's *Bolero*, and Alexander Borodin's *Overture to Prince Igor*. The three following performances of Dawson's symphony on November 16, 17, and 20 were part of the Philadelphia Orchestra's regular season, two taking place at the

Academy of Music and the last at Carnegie Hall in New York. The program for these three concerts featured an array of newer works: American composer Harl McDonald's first symphony, *The Santa Fe Trail*; *Chapultepec*, by Mexican conductor and composer Manuel M. Ponce, and Maurice Ravel's *Rapsodie espagnole*. Stokowski's conception of the *Negro Folk Symphony* and its composer as lying outside of the White, Austro-German classical mainstream is evident in these programming choices.

Dawson's audience-pleasing work concluded each of the last three concerts. Not only did it receive thunderous applause at the end, but at every performance there was an ovation after the second movement's dramatic close. This impressed critic Pitts Sanborn, who described the scene: "Without further ado let it be recorded that Mr. Dawson's 'Negro Folk Symphony' took the house by storm. The custom of no applause during a symphony gave way after the second movement to a spontaneous outburst that brought the orchestra to its feet, and at the end the enthusiasm was so great that Mr. Dawson was called to the stage repeatedly to bow his acknowledgements."[8]

The experience of these first performances and their clamorous reception was not limited to those with concert tickets. The November 16 concert was heard over the Columbia Broadcasting System, reaching radio listeners as far away as Los Angeles. Among the listeners were many African Americans who took a special interest in Dawson's symphonic debut. A letter by listener Mae Belle Thomas represents the tone of dozens more:

> I couldn't decide whether to sit or stand, I was so happy to hear your composition being played. . . . When the applause commenced at the end of the second movement, I applauded with the rest. I hope the student body had an opportunity to hear it, because if they didn't, they missed a great event in every Negro's life. When the announcer said you were on the stage with Mr. Stokowski, I hoped you would say a word. Mr. Dawson, I'm so full of enthusiasm, I can't gather my thoughts correctly. But I must thank you for the million and one Negroes who missed hearing your symphony and again for the thousands that did hear it. It is the greatest contribution of the Negro to the musical world.[9]

In addition to the many friends, acquaintances, colleagues, students, and distant well-wishers who wrote to congratulate Dawson, a number of noteworthy African American musicians sent telegrams, including soprano Caterina Jarboro, choral director and composer Hall Johnson, and composers William Grant Still and Clarence Cameron White.

Professional music critics, too, were largely positive in their response. The *New York Post*'s Samuel Chotzinoff valued the work most for the moments where its uniqueness—and, indeed, its racial "otherness"—was on display:

I suppose the evening's most authentic novelty was Mr. William Dawson's "Negro Folk Symphony," a work based upon Negro folk music and orchestrated with a certain barbarity. . . . The thematic material of the symphony could have been, I thought, more distinguished, and its development less regular and in the "white" tradition. But every now and then there was an outburst of originality and an intimation of a personal approach, or there was a flash of inspiration, as at the thrice-repeated crescendo at the finish of the second movement, with its fatalistic suggestion of the tom-tom.[10]

Leonard Liebling of the *New York American* also praised the work's fresh voice, noting that "Dawson's musical speech, based on Negro spirituals, disdains the European tonal alphabet and patterns, and localizes his material by means of admittedly Southern meters, harmonies and colorings. He does not distort the native simplicity of the spirituals by making them into contrapuntal jigsaws, variations or the concluding fuge [*sic*] so beloved of the composer whose inventiveness peters out before he reaches the logical end of his opus." Unlike Chotzinoff, who found fault with Dawson's adherence to "'white' tradition," Liebling concluded that the *Negro Folk Symphony* was "the most distinctive and promising American symphonic proclamation which has so far been achieved."[11] Returning to Dawson's achievement in an end-of-the-year retrospective for 1934, Liebling surely warmed the composer's heart when he wrote, "Maybe Dvořák's dictum is to be proved correct after all, that great American music is to find its source of inspiration in the Negro and Indian folk material and character."[12]

Reviewers readily noticed that Dawson's symphony bore a family resemblance to Dvořák's *New World Symphony*, commenting sometimes with approval and other times critically. Winthrop Sargeant wrote in the *Brooklyn Daily Eagle* in 1934 that the work was "reminiscent of Dvořák. In fact one of the principal themes of [Dawson's] last movement would make a 'tune detective's' mouth water while he rushed for the score of the New World Symphony."[13] Some, such as the critic for *Musical America*, assumed that Dawson had passively absorbed the European's original ideas: "The influence of Dvořák is strong almost to the point of quotation."[14] As will be seen, Dawson's engagement with the European's famous symphony was far from passive.

Noteworthy praise came from the prominent Black intellectual Alain Locke, who was inspired to add a postscript to his two-part essay in *Opportunity*, "Toward a Critique of Negro Music." Locke heard Dawson's work as serendipitously offering an "answer to the main challenge of this article" by being both distinctively Black and of indisputable quality. (Locke's notion of musical quality owed much to the Germanocentric aesthetics widely shared by the musical elite in the United

States.) Like Liebling, he understood Dvořák as having pointed the way for Dawson's achievement:

> It is moments like this that I had in mind in writing that the truly Negro music must reflect the folk spirit and eventually epitomize the race experience. To have done this without too much programistic literalness is an achievement and points as significant a path to the Negro musician as was pointed by Dvořák years ago. In fact it is the same path, only much further down the road to native and indigenous musical expression. Deep appreciation is due Mr. Stokowski for his discerning vision and masterful interpretation, but great praise is due Mr. Dawson for pioneering achievement in the right direction. His future and that of Negro music is brighter because of it.[15]

In December 1934, Locke sent Dawson a typed draft of this postscript along with a warm letter. He describes having listened "with great pride and satisfaction" to the radio broadcast and concludes by urging the composer to write a concerto or symphony that could feature their "great mutual friend Miss Hazel Harrison" on piano. Like many others, including Dawson himself, Locke imagined that the *Negro Folk Symphony* was only a beginning.

The *Negro Folk Symphony* after 1934

There were only two copies of the full score of the *Negro Folk Symphony*, and one set of orchestral parts. This scarcity was exacerbated when one of the two conductor's scores spent most of 1935 in the hands of the judges for the Juilliard School's Annual Competition for the Publication of Orchestral Compositions. (The *Negro Folk Symphony*, a finalist for the prize, was eventually bested by Albert Elkus's now-forgotten *Reflections from a Greek Tragedy*.) Although conductors including Pierre Monteux and Otto Klemperer indicated their interest in programming the symphony, they had to plan their seasons well in advance, and Dawson could not guarantee that the score and parts would be available at the right time. In the end, only two orchestras actually performed the work in the period immediately following the premiere: the Philadelphia Orchestra under the baton of William Van Den Burg during the 1935 outdoor summer series, and the Birmingham Civic Symphony in Alabama, conducted by Dorsey Whittington in 1935 and 1936. By 1937, the conductors who might have programmed Dawson's piece had apparently forgotten about it.[16]

The *Negro Folk Symphony* was seldom performed until the 1960s. In 1952–53, Dawson fulfilled a lifelong dream by spending several weeks in West Africa (a trip detailed in chapter 5), where he listened to and recorded a wide variety of music-making. Afterward, inspired by his experiences, he undertook a significant revision of his symphony. Stokowski chose to record the revised symphony in 1963 (see Discography), the centennial of the Emancipation Proclamation, making it the first LP released by his new American Symphony Orchestra. Taking advantage of the renewed interest generated by the high-profile recording, in 1965 Dawson entered into an agreement with Shawnee Press for distribution and rental of the score and parts, and had several hundred miniature study scores printed. He was actively involved in efforts to promote the piece among conductors, making a number of suggestions to Shawnee Press about how to publicize the availability of the score. The correspondence shows that the press created a brochure, advocated for window displays at music stores, wrote to conductors, and took other actions in response to Dawson's persistent and sometimes repeated urging.[17]

These efforts resulted in moderate attention and some performances, including at least three that Dawson himself was invited to conduct, by the Kansas City Philharmonic in January 1966, the Baltimore Symphony Orchestra in May 1975, and the Birmingham (Alabama) Symphony Orchestra in February 1976. Consistent interest continued to elude the *Negro Folk Symphony*, however. The American classical establishment remained Eurocentric and conservative; on the rare occasions when an orchestra saw fit to program a Black composer, William Grant Still's appealing *Afro-American Symphony* was often the default choice. Additionally, Dawson's score and parts remained relatively difficult to acquire and work with, as chapter 5 will show.

Perhaps also a factor, the term "Negro" began to fall out of favor in the mid-1960s, as many members of the race came to prefer "Black" and, later, "African American." To this day, the title *Negro Folk Symphony* can raise eyebrows and cause discomfort. In March 2022, the Fort Worth Symphony Orchestra performed the piece with the title *Folk Symphony*. For the Brevard Music Center Orchestra's concert in July 2022, the piece was listed as *Symphony No. 1*. Chineke! Orchestra used the title *African-American Folk Symphony* for its August 2022 performances in Europe. Given Dawson's desire to inscribe race indelibly on his symphony ("Can't remove that title!"), Chineke! Orchestra's approach seems to offer the best balance of respect for the composer's intention and sensitivity to changes in language use.[18] That said, up until his passing in 1990 Dawson never showed any interest in adjusting the title to reflect the times, and it is difficult to imagine that he would welcome these changes today.

Between 1965 and 2020, the total number of performances was only in the low dozens. Recordings followed Stokowski's at the rate of one every thirty years or so: one by the Detroit Symphony Orchestra in 1993, conducted by Neeme Järvi, and one by the Vienna Radio Symphony Orchestra under the baton of Arthur Fagen in 2020 (see Discography). The scarcity of recordings not only provided evidence of the symphony's neglect but also likely contributed to it, as the shortcomings of the 1963 and 1993 recordings may have discouraged conductors from programming the piece. Stokowski's American Symphony Orchestra turns in a performance that is rough-edged in intonation and ensemble playing. The tempos are sometimes slower than what Dawson indicated in the score; for example, the introduction, marked at sixty-three beats per minute, never exceeds fifty. The recording does have its strengths; for instance, the timbres of the individual instruments and sections can be heard with admirable clarity, and the percussion parts are suitably prominent. The performance is palpably sincere, befitting Stokowski's return to the *Negro Folk Symphony* during the Civil Rights Era. It is unclear how much influence Dawson had on the interpretation or what he thought of the recording, though surely he was pleased that Stokowski chose his symphony for his new orchestra's first LP. A photograph on the record's back cover shows the composer and conductor examining the score together; one hopes that their interaction went well beyond this photo opportunity (figure 4.1).

Figure 4.1. Dawson and Leopold Stokowski, ca. 1963. Tuskegee University Archives.

The performance on the Detroit Symphony Orchestra album is technically superb, and the recording quality of the 1993 release is sumptuous. Unfortunately the brisk tempos taken by Järvi in the outer movements sometimes deprive this thematically, texturally, and emotionally dense music of its full impact and even at times, in the last movement, of its comprehensibility. This failing becomes apparent when one listens to the recording released in 2020 by the Vienna Radio Symphony Orchestra under the baton of Arthur Fagen. A deeply sympathetic rendition that combines Stokowski's sincerity with Järvi's sonic lushness and virtuosity, it allows the music to breathe as well as to surge forward. The middle movement is particularly effective, the anguish of its outer sections brought into harrowing relief by the frolicsome central episode. This recording has won Dawson's piece many new admirers.[19]

The early 2020s have seen an unprecedented surge in performances and recordings of the *Negro Folk Symphony*, as the Black Lives Matter movement has led orchestras to reconsider the White, Eurocentric status quo of their programming and to seek out works by composers from marginalized groups. After having been used only once or twice per year for decades, the score and parts of Dawson's symphony were rented four times in 2020, six in 2021, and thirty in 2022, by ensembles ranging from collegiate, regional, and summer festival orchestras to major professional symphony orchestras in the United States and abroad.[20] The *Negro Folk Symphony* is generating great enthusiasm among the conductors now discovering it. Says James Blachly, whose organization performed the work in May 2022: "The first time I conducted William Levi Dawson's *Negro Folk Symphony* with Experiential Orchestra was also the first time that every single member of the orchestra had ever performed the piece. For all of us, it was a revelation. . . . I believe it can be convincingly argued that this is the greatest symphony by an American composer."[21] Professional recordings are now proliferating, including by the Royal Scottish National Orchestra in 2022 (conducted by Kellen Gray) and Seattle Symphony in 2023 (Roderick Cox). Several videos of full concert performances by professional and student orchestras are available on YouTube. A long-needed new performing edition by the present author was issued by G. Schirmer in 2023; soon after, the first recording using the score was made by conductor Yannick Nézet-Séguin and the Philadelphia Orchestra, the ensemble that premiered the piece almost ninety years before. It is to be hoped that the new edition and critical mass of excellent recordings will continue the dramatic upward trajectory of the *Negro Folk Symphony*, securing for it at last the prominence it has long deserved.

Music and Meaning

In the *Negro Folk Symphony*, several musical worlds are placed in dynamic tension. Fundamentally the piece engages with the European symphonic tradition despite the active discouragement from doing so that Dawson faced during his studies in Kansas City and Chicago. His symphony amply demonstrates his rightful place as a practitioner of the genre, while it also shows him grappling with the tradition—most directly, with Dvořák's *New World Symphony*, that beloved, romanticized vision of the New World. Dawson's work emerges not only as a worthy contribution to the symphonic canon, but as a necessary, corrective one.

The *Negro Folk Symphony* does not begin with an obvious folk melody, and aside from using a pentatonic scale, the introduction eschews the markers of Blackness that Dawson's audience might expect, such as syncopated rhythm or a bluesy slide (à la George Gershwin's *Rhapsody in Blue*). Rather, the composer clearly signals from the start that this work is in conversation with Dvořák's *New World Symphony*. Anyone familiar with the earlier work will easily hear its echoes in Dawson's. His choice of instrumentation, scales, harmonic language, texture, and mood all call Dvořák to mind as effectively as could anything short of actual quotation. (It is worth noting that the first symphonies of William Grant Still and Florence B. Price are also in conversation with this work, as scholars including Rae Linda Brown and Douglas W. Shadle have discussed.[22])

In one sense, the *Negro Folk Symphony* pays a kind of homage to Dvořák and his *New World Symphony*. Dawson made no secret of their importance to himself as a composer. Throughout his life, Dawson proudly noted that his hero (and acquaintance) Harry T. Burleigh had introduced Dvořák to the African American religious folk songs, and was buoyed by the Bohemian composer's 1893 declaration that "the future music of [the United States] must be founded upon what are called the negro [*sic*] melodies."[23] Dawson's copy of the *New World Symphony* score, purchased during his Kansas City years (1922–25), contains notations in pencil that reflect his close study of that work's form, thematic content, and harmonic structure, and also indicate his admiration for the beauty and effectiveness of certain passages. (An image from that score is reproduced in figure 4.4.)[24]

And yet, while the *Negro Folk Symphony* is a respectful troping of Dvořák's 9th Symphony, it can at the same time be heard as implicitly critical of the earlier symphony, illuminating through contrast how Dvořák's music remains on the surface, providing an outsider's perspective on the New World's landscape and inhabitants. Dvořák presents an expertly paced series of almost scenic pleasures; by contrast, Dawson allows his themes to flex and contract unpredictably across the timeline, telling a story that is dynamic, complex, and marked by Dawson's individuality. The *Negro Folk Symphony* does not daub "Negro folk" color onto a Dvořákian symphonic model that is already complete without it. Rather, by imbuing his symphony with his own idiosyncratic Black voice, Dawson shines a light on the absence of a non-White subjectivity from Dvořák's work.

The *Negro Folk Symphony* is no less deeply engaged with the musical worlds of Dawson's Black ancestors than with European symphonic precedents. Composing the symphony in the late 1920s, Dawson turned to African American religious folk songs for thematic material, an approach that was paradoxically both traditional and radical. On the one hand, European composers had long drawn on folk music for nationalist and exoticist purposes. The "spirituals" themselves had been sung and played in concert arrangements since the 1870s, and their use as themes for instrumental music had already been pioneered by Dvořák and others, including Dawson's composition teacher Thorvald Otterström. On the other hand, for a Black composer for whom slavery was recent family history, and whose understanding of African American music and spirituality was bone deep, the implications of bringing the subjectivity of the enslaved with him into the concert hall were radical indeed. Dawson built into his symphony not simply the melodies of the folk songs but the experiences to which the songs bear witness, and the pain, faith, and determination that they express.

It is tempting to hear the *Negro Folk Symphony* as a product of the Harlem Renaissance of the 1920s and '30s, given the timing of its composition and the ways in which it resonates with Renaissance themes such as race pride and nationalism.[25] However, Dawson never expressed an affinity for the movement, and he certainly did not share the perspective of Alain Locke and others that African American folk culture needed to be vindicated through transformation into serious art.[26] Moreover, many of the symphony's most politically and aesthetically provocative elements were incorporated in Dawson's revision of the work years after the Renaissance, inspired by his visit to West Africa in 1952–53. Experiencing the music of his ancestors' homeland equipped him to unsettle the nineteenth-century European aesthetics that had been his touchstone in the 1920s.

One change that Dawson made over the decades was to a key element of his symphony's program, which traces the journey of a people from Africa (the first movement is titled "The Bond of Africa"), through the sufferings of slavery (the second movement, "Hope in the Night"), and into a hopeful present or possibly future (the third movement, "O Le' Me Shine!"). Threaded through all three movements is a recurring four-note "Leading Motive" which, in 1934, he described as "symbolic of the link uniting Africa and her rich heritage with her descendants in America."[27] Almost thirty years later, the liner notes to Stokowski's LP characterize the motive's meaning less euphemistically: "In the composer's view, 'a link was taken out of a human chain when the first African was taken from the shores of his native land and sent to slavery.' The solemn motive of the Introduction, first sounded by the French horn, symbolizes this 'missing link.'"[28] The more pointed language suggests that Dawson was politically energized in this period; he reportedly participated in one of the pivotal civil rights marches from Selma to Montgomery two years later, in 1965.[29]

The *Negro Folk Symphony* is both a monumental statement and a very personal one. The descriptive analysis in the coming pages, in addition to examining basic elements such as form and program, also follows the revised symphony's complex interwoven threads—those of the European symphony (especially Dvořák's 9th Symphony), the African American religious folk song, and West African drumming as the composer experienced it in the early 1950s. Manipulating these threads confidently and deliberately, Dawson creates a Signifyin(g) tour de force. Horace J. Maxile Jr. explains the challenge such a work poses to full understanding: "The signifying process . . . is both dynamic (musical figures commenting on other musical figures) and intertextual (musical figures commenting on themselves). One must be adept with both the signifier and the signified in order to discuss the referential richness of this process and to recognize varying levels of topical signification in structural and expressive domains."[30]

No single analysis can exhaust the "referential richness" of the *Negro Folk Symphony*. Considering its exceptional quality, the remarkable breadth of cultural materials from which it draws, and the depth of its composer's knowledge and understanding of those materials, this work has been woefully under-examined; the present effort is only the third substantial analysis it has received. Far more in this richly intertextual masterpiece remains to be explored.[31]

I. The Bond of Africa

Dawson begins his engagement with European symphonic tradition and African American religious folk song from the very beginning of the *Negro Folk Symphony*. The opening phrase, sounded by the solo horn, is arresting but mysterious: unharmonized, rhythmically unpredictable, neither plaintive nor militant.

Figure 4.2. Dawson, Basic Thematic Material of the *Negro Folk Symphony*. William Levi Dawson Papers, series 2, box 10, folder 1. Reproduced by permission of the Milton L. Randolph Jr. Estate.

(The phrase can be found in the first line of the "Basic Thematic Material" sketch, figure 4.2.) The first four notes comprise the Link Motive heard throughout the symphony, whose programmatic meaning Dawson revised between 1934 and 1963 (although he left the first measures of the symphony unaltered). Distinctive aspects of the motive include its intervals, descending contour, and concluding short-long rhythm, sometimes referred to as the "Scotch snap." These resemble the intervals, contour, and rhythm found in some versions of the African American folk song *Go Down, Moses*, at the words "Egypt's land" (figure 4.3).

It is possible that the resemblance is a coincidence.[32] If intentional, the subtlety of the allusion calls to mind Dvořák's paraphrase of *Swing Low, Sweet Chariot* in his first movement's secondary theme in the *New World Symphony*, which Dawson labeled in his copy of the score (figure 4.4). Unlike the three folk songs Dawson names as thematic sources in his program notes, he does not identify *Go Down, Moses* as a source for the Link Motive. The first phrase of the *Negro Folk Symphony* is not meant to be easily interpreted, whether as a quotation or as expressing an unambiguous emotion or idea.

Immediately after the first phrase come three responding phrases whose moods are much easier to interpret: first grim agreement, then grief, then tragic grandeur. Each phrase flows out of the last. The opening phrase then sounds again, played by the unaccompanied English horn. That instrument's plaintive timbre, combined with the affect of the phrases just heard, allows the listener to interpret the formerly inscrutable phrase, which now emerges as lonely and sorrowful. By taking a phrase that at first seemed purely mythic and revealing it as personal and expressive, Dawson Signifies on the enthusiastic outsider's perspective on the New World found in Dvořák's symphony. The Adagio introduction of the *Negro Folk Symphony* boldly evokes the grandeur of the famous earlier work's introduction while also intimating that Dawson's New World

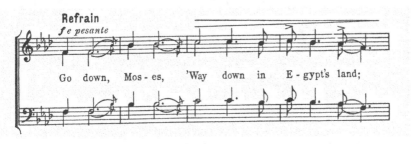

Figure 4.3. *Go Down, Moses*, mm. 8–12. Dett, *Religious Folk Songs of the Negro*, 108.

Figure 4.4. From Dawson's copy of Antonín Dvořák, *Symphonie Number Five: Aus der neuen Welt* (Berlin: N. Simrock, 1903). William Levi Dawson Papers, series 9, box 115, folder 5. Reproduced by permission of the Milton L. Randolph Jr. Estate.

will not be shown from a comfortably scenic vantage point, but with a Black subjectivity, from within.

At the tempo shift from the introductory *Adagio* to the *Allegro con brio* of the first movement's exposition, Dawson again invites comparison to the parallel moment in Dvořák's 9th Symphony, similarly using a string tremolo backdrop to support a heroic horn melody. Aside from this texture and instrumentation, however, Dawson departs significantly from the earlier work. Whereas the rhythm of Dvořák's primary theme is succinct and energetic, Dawson's alternates unpredictable long notes and bouncy syncopated ones (figure 4.2, first movement theme "a"). Dvořák's melody is almost entirely triadic, whereas Dawson's is chromatic and blues-inflected, including both the major and minor 3rd scale degrees and the flat 7th. Dawson's theme also, most strikingly, twice places a strong emphasis on the unusual raised 5th scale degree (B-natural), each time lingering on the note for several beats before resolving it down to the "normal" 5th. In emphasizing an unexpected note in a symphonic first movement's primary theme, Dawson calls to mind another famous European symphony: Beethoven's 3rd, the *Eroica*. (Perhaps coincidentally, both pieces are in E-flat major.) As in that work, the surprising note has implications that play out over the rest of the symphony.

Dawson subsequently handles his un-Dvořákian primary theme in a thoroughly un-Dvořákian manner, immediately compressing and developing it along with the Leading Motive, hurtling through a series of rhythmic and harmonic adventures. Not until the arrival of the contrasting second theme (m. 145; figure 4.2, first movement theme "b") does Dawson finally provide the kind of music that one would likely expect of a work titled *Negro Folk Symphony*: a memorable tune with predictable phrase lengths, triadic harmony, and lively syncopation in the accompaniment. This theme is closely based on a folk song, *Oh, My Little Soul Gwine Shine Like a Star*, better known as *Dig My Grave* (shown in figure 4.5 in Dawson's hand). The melody features a raised 4th scale degree, mirroring the first theme's unexpected note a half step *above* the 5th scale degree. The respite from motivic development and rhythmic complexity that the second theme provides lasts only eighteen measures. At measure (m.) 163, a new theme is introduced that is almost purely rhythmic in character, consisting of a motoric repeated figure evoking the Link Motive's Scotch snap. George Jellinek's 1963 LP liner notes describe this passage as "strongly animated and suggestive of rhythmic hand-clapping."[33] Incorporating fragments of the second theme's folk song, the section builds to an exciting rhythmic climax.

The onset of the central development section at m. 221 is heralded by the Link Motive, sounded ominously in canon by trombones, horns, trumpets, English

Figure 4.5. Dawson, sketch of folk song, *Oh, My Little Soul Gwine Shine Like a Star*. William Levi Dawson Papers, series 2, box 137, folder 4. Reproduced by permission of the Milton L. Randolph Jr. Estate.

horn, and clarinets. Dawson manages to make the development section stand out from the already heavily developmental previous section, virtuosically manipulating the Link Motive and themes from the exposition. He unleashes unpredictable tempo changes and forceful rhythms and polyrhythms along with a level of dissonance that puts to rest any lingering expectations of folk simplicity. The fourteen measures that lead up to the recapitulation (starting at m. 378) presage the walking tempo and somber mood of the slow movement to come, repeating the rhythm of the Link Motive over a pulsing B-natural in the low strings. This note, a half-step away from the B-flat one might expect to find at this point in sonata form (the 5th scale degree in E-flat major), connects back to the unexpected, emphasized B-natural at the start of the exposition. It also foreshadows the unexpected B minor key of the coming second movement.

The recapitulation section begins at m. 392 with familiar tempo, texture, and motives from the exposition, but in another unexpected key, G-flat major. The move from B to G-flat resembles the descending fourth (B to "F#") of a blues progression, IV to I, rather than the traditional European V to I. E-flat does not return as a tonal center until a powerful blast of E-flat minor (m. 418) as the first theme sounds against a barrage of quarter-note triplets. Polyrhythms, Scotch snaps, and blue notes (especially the flat 3rd and 6th scale degrees) become increasingly prevalent as the recapitulation proceeds. The low instruments come to the fore in an ominous slow passage (mm. 454–64) whose bass line wends its way downward by step to hold an extremely quiet (*ppppp*) F before the coda begins at m. 465 (*Agitato e staccatissimo*). The note C-flat (B-natural, enharmonically spelled) at the start of this section is again emphasized; this time it progresses according to European harmonic practice, moving down a half step to B-flat and then resolving to E-flat, the tonic of the piece. The folk song-based second theme, having been absent from the recapitulation proper, makes its delayed appearance (at m. 489) with triumphant instrumentation that makes brilliant use of the piccolo. As the coda builds to its final climactic cadences, Dawson layers the folk theme and the first theme in a rhythmically kaleidoscopic texture. Instead of alternating tonic and dominant chords, the movement ends with the tonic chord vying with the submediant C-flat major chord, showing that this disruptive note has not yet been put to rest.

II. Hope in the Night

The powerful second movement, in a conventional but not formulaic ABA form, has been successfully programmed as a stand-alone piece since 1935. It has the most specific program of the symphony's movements, starting from the opening three gong strokes, "symbol of the Trinity that guides the destiny of man." The first of the movement's three sections features a plodding accompaniment in the strings and harp, "suggesting the monotonous life of people who were held in bondage for two hundred and fifty years." There is nothing idyllic or nostalgic in this portrait of antebellum life. For the first several measures the strings alternate between B minor, the key of the movement (a significant note, as discussed above), and G major. These two chords are closely related, so that motion between them is harmonically uneventful, even "monotonous." (G also bears the same relationship to B that the note B bears to E-flat, mirroring the first movement's emphasis on the raised 5th or lowered 6th scale degree.)

Above the trudging string accompaniment, "the English horn sings a plaintive lament, a plea from the darkness" (figure 4.2, second movement). Again Dawson invites comparison with Dvořák's *New World Symphony*, whose famous Adagio theme is also first "sung" by a solo English horn. Once again, the contrast is striking. Whereas Dvořák wrote a pentatonic melody so lovely that William Arms Fisher turned it into the popular faux spiritual *Goin' Home*, Dawson's melody resists being heard as an archetypal "folk" statement. Although it is a lyrical melody with a conventional 8-bar phrase structure, it incorporates chromaticism, rhythmic surprises (including the Scotch snap), and a contour that rises and falls unpredictably. This melody does not present an aestheticized, generalized, "Negro folk" suffering for White listeners to pity and enjoy. Rather, Dawson's distinctive melody conveys a suffering that was endured by millions of individuals. This is the only movement in the symphony that does not incorporate a named religious folk song, thus withholding the comfort the listener might otherwise derive from the idea of the enslaved finding solace in their singing.

A full orchestral climax beginning at m. 31 combines the main melody (altered to include a prominent tritone) with a grimly descending chromatic accompaniment and a low ostinato reminiscent of the Link Motive. After reaching this "pitch of desperation," as the program calls it, the movement's middle section commences in a contrasting "*alla scherzando*" mood. The harrowing climax just past renders the shift more of a jolt than a relief. The section "symbolizes the merry play of children, yet unaware of the hopelessness beclouding their future." A jaunty new tune in D major, derived from the Leading Motive, recalls the spirit of the secondary theme of the first movement but without reference to any named folk song. Dissonance creeps steadily in until at last the Link Motive returns in a merciless burst from the full orchestra (mm. 102–4). The passage that follows is perhaps the most devastating of the symphony: a small collection of solo strings and winds perform desolate shreds of the first section's English horn theme, then the solo cello climbs alone to a keening high F above middle C before subsiding slowly down into the return at m. 118 of the key, texture, and melody from the beginning of the movement.

At this point the listener likely perceives the commencement of the third section in a straightforward ABA structure, with the contrasting middle section having substituted for what would have been a separate scherzo movement in a four-movement symphony. However, this is not even the movement's halfway mark. What seems at first to be the return of the A section turns out to be only a brief episode amidst an ongoing B section. After seven measures the "*alla scherzando*" melody returns, with turbulent shifting tempos, sophisticated polyphony (including an inverted canon), and fragmented themes from the A and B sections as well as the Link Motive. Another orchestral climax occurs at m. 175, convulsing on a cacophonous eight-note chord with brass flutter-tonguing and harp glissando.

What emerges shortly after this crisis, at m. 184, is a deeply emotional, Romantic, full-throated orchestral statement of the movement's opening melody in B *major*, with tolling chimes and the melody presented in canon. This is where the third section of the ABA form actually begins. The heroic mood is short-lived, and after a climax of stunning dissonance at m. 198 (where the quarter notes begin in the double bass part), the opening "monotonous" music returns one last time at m. 208, the English horn reprising its role but now in counterpoint with the solo flute playing a slow, metrically off-kilter version of the children's formerly playful theme. After a few forcefully interrupting returns of the Leading Motive, the movement seems to be reaching its conclusion with a quiet new theme (starting at m. 230) played in unison by the violas, cellos, and double basses, clearly derived from the Leading Motive and evocative of that motive's ambiguous character when heard at the start of the symphony.

This seeming conclusion, however, is in the wrong key: G minor. The lowered 6th scale degree has been important throughout the symphony, and as he did in the first movement, Dawson uses it in place of the expected 5th scale degree as the root of the last chord before the final tonic chord. At m. 235, the low strings simply shift to the correct key of B minor—a move that is startling to the analyst but not the listener, for whom the sparse texture and quiet dynamic level render the shift gentle on the ear.

The final twenty-two measures of the "Hope in the Night" movement are unprecedented in symphonic literature. Once the harmony reaches the final B minor chord in m. 238, it remains there for what, at Dawson's notated tempo of quarter note = 69, amounts to well over a minute. (The conductor Arthur Fagen, who recorded the symphony in 2020, was the first to follow Dawson's score faithfully here. The effect is stunning.) Although the harmony comes to a protracted standstill, every other parameter of the music remains active. Three times, a gong stroke is followed by a richly orchestrated B minor chord that proceeds from very quiet to very loud and back again, accompanied by an unwavering tenor drum pulse. Each chord is longer than the previous one, and as the last fades to nothingness the tenor drum continues its inexorable pulse, keeping a consistent tempo while fading to a dynamic marking of *ppppp*. The devastating impact of this conclusion is not unlike that of Tchaikovsky's last symphony, the *Pathétique*, a score Dawson owned.

The 1963 liner notes describe this conclusion: "The movement closes with three strikes of the gong followed by solemn crescendos and decrescendos, recalling the mysterious mood of the opening, as the tom-tom beats relentlessly, sounding the note of bleak, unvarying monotony, dying away in the distance." Dawson depicts slavery through the eyes of those held in bondage, as a day-to-day experience that would be endured by one's children and by countless generations to come. The movement's keynote turns out not to be the first word of the title, "Hope in the Night," but the last: hope does not shine in the night, but rather is engulfed by it.

III. O Le' Me Shine, Shine Like a Morning Star!

The third movement demonstrates beyond a doubt Dawson's abundant mastery of the resources of the symphony orchestra and the symphonic genre. It also prominently includes elements derived from both African American and West African musical practices. Virtuosically weaving together "Negro folk" and "symphony," the movement offers a symbolic, musical repair of the break in the human chain wrought by the transatlantic slave trade.

After the crushing sadness of the second movement, the third begins with a gentle ray of hope, as solo wind instruments call to each other over a shimmering string tremolo. This texture, combined with the second wind instrument's entry a perfect fourth below the first, calls to mind the opening of the last movement of Beethoven's Symphony No. 6, the *Pastoral*, another score in Dawson's possession, which programmatically depicts shepherds giving thanks after a storm. An optimistic motive is passed from solo woodwind to woodwind (figure 4.2, third movement theme "a"). This four-note motive with a Scotch snap is related to the Link Motive while also quoting the African American folk song that provides the movement's title (figure 4.6). Surprisingly the first conclusive cadence (at m. 27) is not in E-flat major but in G minor, suggesting that the previous movement's bleakness is not yet forgotten.

The second theme, based on the African American folk song *Hallelujah, Lord, I Been Down into the Sea* (figure 4.2, third movement theme "b"; see also figure 4.7,), appears at m. 86 played by a choir of wind instruments sounding much like an organ. This melody has been hinted at during the very active, developmental pre-

Figure 4.6. Dawson, sketch of folk song, *Oh, Le' Me Shine*. William Levi Dawson Papers, series 2, box 137, folder 4. Reproduced by permission of the Milton L. Randolph Jr. Estate.

Figure 4.7. Dawson, sketch of folk song, *Hallelujah, Lord, I Been Down into the Sea*. William Levi Dawson Papers, series 2, box 137, folder 4. Reproduced by permission of the Milton L. Randolph Jr. Estate.

ceding passage, so that when it receives its spotlighted appearance here it feels like both a culmination and a moment of calm. The song's text is rich in meaning, with themes of baptism and renewal, challenges overcome ("I've been to the sea, and I've done been tried"), and escape across or through water, a concept found in many African American religious folk songs including *Wade in the Water* and *Deep River*. The second theme appears in G major, replacing the tragic G minor heard earlier. G is also exactly as far above the key note of E-flat as the earlier "problem" note of B/C-flat was below it, providing harmonic symmetry.

The third movement proceeds through the expected exposition, development, and recapitulation of sonata form. Dawson skillfully manipulates his melodic materials, as the two folk song–derived themes intertwine with the Link Motive. Over the course of the movement the music grows increasingly complex, with mounting fragmentation, dissonance, polyphony, call-and-response, polyrhythms, and metric displacement. Dawson manipulates themes and motives until their boundaries blur, as in the oboe part at mm. 116–9, where the second theme expands so that the second half of it becomes a version of the Link Motive.

The conclusion of the symphony can be heard as giving the last word to Africa.[34] After one final C-flat chord (actually an augmented sixth chord), returning one more time to the flat 6th scale degree and using it again as a substitute for the dominant chord, at m. 483 Dawson lands on the final tonic E-flat major chord. Drawing on his experiences of drumming in West Africa, he allows the percussion section (greatly expanded in the revised symphony, with the metal clave and xylophone heard only here) to dominate the texture with intense, interlocking rhythms. The string section, too, becomes rhythmically dense. Particularly interesting is the prominent timpani, which imitates the West African talking drum throughout this passage. After a grand pause during which the timpani sounds a short descending motive three times, the whole orchestra finishes the piece by playing a four-note motive in unison: the home note of E-flat twice, and then the 5th scale degree twice.

Like that of the second movement, this conclusion is unprecedented. Using the full orchestra to declaim a motive derived from West African drumming and first articulated by the timpani, Dawson transforms what Stokowski called "the white man's most highly developed instrument, the symphony orchestra" into a drum.[35] The composer abandons the virtually universal practice in European tonal music of ending with the key note of the piece. The concluding four-note gesture also provides a remarkable "response" to the Link Motive's four-note "call," first sounded by the horn at the start of the symphony. That opening gesture was rhythmically jagged and unpredictable, performed by a lone instrument, fatalistically descending, and harmonically outlined a C minor chord. The four-note concluding response, by contrast, is rhythmically decisive, fully orchestrated, expansive (some instruments go up from E-flat to B-flat, others go down), and nontriadic. If the Leading Motive represented the severed link between Black Americans and Africa, this conclusion celebrates their reconnection—something that Dawson had experienced literally and personally in 1952–53.

The barrage of percussion does not render harmony irrelevant or subsidiary. The concluding celebratory explosion features the notes of an E-flat major pentatonic scale: E-flat, F, G, B-flat, and C. The phrase that opened the piece used this same collection, with C as the key note. The three most emphasized pitches in the concluding passage are E-flat, B-flat, and—unexpectedly—not G (the third member of the tonic triad) but F. The last held chord, cut off before the final drum gesture, consists of these three notes. One can hear this sonority as a quartal harmony or a subset of the pentatonic collection. It is decidedly not an E-flat major triad.

In his *Negro Folk Symphony* Dawson combines African, African American, and European musical materials in order to write a Black subjectivity into a prestigious concert hall genre. Throughout the work, Dawson conveys both his own artistic sensibility and his deep empathy for the experiences of his ancestors. He does this by avoiding simplistic markers of Black cultures (whether African or African American), instead weaving those musics into a conspicuously complex and brilliant symphonic structure. He refers—sometimes quite frankly—to symphonies by Dvořák, Tchaikovsky, and Beethoven to claim his symphony's place among theirs, and his own place among those composers. He insists throughout the *Negro Folk Symphony* on a depiction of African American experience that is rooted in the individual and collective humanity of Black people. He steers carefully clear of music that could be heard as formulaic or romanticizing, favoring chromaticism, churning development, and complex textures and rhythms. Even though the seeds of this finale are present in the very first notes of the work, it takes three movements of struggle before the composer offers the kinetic, percussive, pentatonic music that a piece titled *Negro Folk Symphony* might have been expected to feature throughout.

It is astonishing that this perfect ending was written decades after the composer originally completed the symphony. The version that the Philadelphia Orchestra first performed in 1934 concluded conventionally, with repeated E-flat major chords in the full orchestra and then a final unison E-flat.[36] The change suggests that Dawson had come to care less about conforming to European symphonic tradition than about expressing his commitment to African heritage and

African American history. (It is surely no coincidence that the piece ends with the sound of drums forbidden to those held in slavery.) The 1950s saw Dawson taking dramatic steps, including his first travels outside of the United States and his resignation from Tuskegee Institute. The *Negro Folk Symphony*'s brilliant revised ending reflects the inspiration Dawson drew from his experiences in Africa, as well as the seasoned musicianship and mature self-confidence that emboldened him to transform a work that had already been a stellar success at its premiere.

Instrumental Works, Before and After

Before the explosive 1934 premiere of his symphony, Dawson composed a variety of works in instrumental genres, none of which he ever saw fit to publish. Responding late in life to the president of Southern Cross Records, who had expressed an interest in his early instrumental pieces, Dawson reminisced briefly about his Chicago composition teacher Adolph Weidig, "who introduced me to the beautiful world of chamber music. . . . At that time, I wrote several pieces in that genre; for many years these have been in storage." He then concluded cryptically, "For this reason and others, I feel that they should remain in peace."[37]

For better or worse, his wishes have largely been granted, and his manuscripts rest—albeit with more frequent visitors of late than in former years—in the William Levi Dawson Papers at Emory University. The exception is his 1927 Sonata for Violin and Piano, an appealing three-movement piece in a folk-inflected, Afro-Romantic style. The central Largo pleased Dawson enough that he created arrangements for piano trio and string quartet. Alone among the early works, the sonata has received a modicum of attention from scholars and performers.[38] George Steel, Abrams Curator of Boston's Isabella Stewart Gardner Museum, commissioned an edition of the quartet version of the *Largo*, which Castle of Our Skins performed movingly in a video presentation in 2021.[39] Steel's commission of a new edition of the full violin sonata was premiered by Randall Goosby and pianist Zhu Wang that same year.

Compositions remaining at rest for now include *Interlude for Orchestra and Piano*, *Adagietto for String Orchestra*, and *Romance in A for Violin, Cello, and Piano*. An orchestral movement titled *Oppression* is an early version of what would become the second movement of the *Negro Folk Symphony*. Dawson also created concert band arrangements of the Black organist Melville Charlton's *Poème Érotique* and of the *Juba* movement from R. Nathaniel Dett's piano suite, *In the Bottoms*. Dawson's early works show him to have been deft with instrumentation, expansively lyrical, rhythmically precise, and highly skilled at both development and counterpoint. His harmonic language was tonal, tastefully chromatic, and only very occasionally influenced by jazz.

In addition to the Rodman Wanamaker awards Dawson won in 1930 and 1931 for his youthful songs *Jump Back, Honey, Jump Back* and *Lovers Plighted*, respectively, in 1930 he also won a Wanamaker Award for an orchestral Scherzo. This work is not to be found in the collection at Emory. Intriguingly a newspaper article about Dawson's symphony, written almost two years before its 1934 premiere, describes it as a four-movement work, the third of which is a Scherzo.[40] It seems plausible that this rejected movement was the award-winning lost piece.

Later, during the *Negro Folk Symphony*'s years of obscurity, Dawson composed one more orchestral work: *A Negro Work Song*. This short piece was commissioned in 1939 for folklorist Alan Lomax's radio program *Folk Music of America*. Part of CBS's American School of the Air educational programming, each episode highlighted a particular genre of folk song (cowboy songs, campfire songs, African American religious folk songs, etc.), including several examples of each genre and culminating with a newly commissioned orchestral work. Among the other composers who received commissions for this program and its successor, *The Wellsprings of America*, were Aaron Copland (*John Henry*), Roy Harris (*Goodbye Old Paint*), Ruth Crawford Seeger (*Rissolty, Rossolty*), Charles Seeger (*John Hardy*), and William Grant Still (*Can't You Line Them?*).[41]

The fifteen-minute episode in which *A Negro Work Song* aired on February 20, 1940, included Huddie "Leadbelly" Ledbetter and the Golden Gate Quartet singing *Rock Island Line, Old Grey Goose*, and *Stewball*.[42] Dawson's commission was based on this last song. In a 1948 letter to the conductor Thor Johnson, Dawson wrote that "the figures which [*Stewball*] contained were not very interesting, which meant that I had to do quite a bit of juggling in order to create something of interest."[43] Nonetheless, he created an effective work. *A Negro Work Song* nods to the style of *Stewball* with bluesy melodies and call-and-response. By contrast, the composition's somber mood, sighing half-step motives, and rich harmony drawing from late Romanticism and jazz are quite distant from the steady, energetic spirit of *Stewball* as sung by Leadbelly and the Golden Gate Quartet. *A Negro Work Song* seems more concerned with the inner life of the laborer than with his song.

The piece was broadcast live again on CBS Radio on March 6, 1943, conducted by Bernard Herrmann. It received at least three performances by orchestras in the South between 1950 and 1954.[44] Then it lay largely forgotten until March 2022, when it enjoyed a well-received revival in Washington, D.C., by the PostClassical Ensemble, conducted by Angel Gil-Ordóñez. It may see publication and further performances in coming years, as the current *Negro Folk Symphony* renaissance continues to bring attention to this and other dormant works by Dawson.

As intriguing as *A Negro Work Song* is, and as worthy as it may be of performance and study, the fact remains that Dawson himself did not love this piece. One can almost hear him uncharacteristically pulling away from the folk song; even immediately after hearing *Stewball* in the radio episode, it is hard to pick it out in *A Negro Work Song*.[45] Dawson's true feelings about this composition are impossible to know. What is unmistakable, however, is the contrast between this work and the *Negro Folk Symphony*, which he cherished and championed throughout his life. In the symphony, as in his masterpieces for choir, Dawson strove to shine the clearest, most dazzling spotlight on African American folk songs that his training and brilliance could summon.

5 | After Tuskegee

WILLIAM L. DAWSON ROUTINELY CORRECTED THOSE who claimed he had retired from Tuskegee Institute in 1955, noting that he had in fact resigned. "Retirement" was indeed an inaccurate term: he continued working for more than three decades after his resignation.

Although his feelings toward Tuskegee Institute in those years were a complicated mixture of pride and resentment, Dawson and his wife Cecile remained lifelong Tuskegee residents. They attended the Washington Chapel AME Church, in whose music ministry Dawson chose not to play a role.[1] Cecile continued as owner and proprietor of the Petite Bazaar into the 1980s, contributing as much as her husband to the household income in some years. In addition to women's clothing and accessories, the shop sold the Tuskegee Institute Choir's *Spirituals* LP (1955) and the 1963 Decca recording of the *Negro Folk Symphony* made by Leopold Stokowski and the American Symphony Orchestra, including by mail order. Cecile occasionally accompanied her husband on his travels to conducting and speaking engagements, as in 1971 when he served as keynote speaker at a conference on Afro-Caribbean music in St. Thomas, Virgin Islands. She also enjoyed going on international tours with her friends, exploring far-flung locations including Japan, Italy, Côte d'Ivoire, and India, sometimes bringing back items to sell in her shop.

Cecile designed the house in which the couple lived after Dawson's resignation, overseeing its construction in 1956 while he was in Spain. The home was thoughtfully decorated, displaying works by Black artists, including their friends Aaron Douglas and Hale Woodruff, alongside many mementos and family photos. Set in the hearth was a stone from the chimney of the house where Booker T. Washington was born, gifted to the composer by Washington's nephew. The Dawsons' guest book shows that the couple entertained frequently between 1957 and 1987; among their guests were visitors from Ghana, Nigeria, Togo, and Brazil, American music scholars Hildred Roach and James Standifer, and the folk singer Odetta. By all accounts, William and Cecile were devoted life partners. They supported one another's efforts, respected each other's independence, and enjoyed a warm, child-free marriage that lasted nearly fifty-five years.

The second half of Dawson's career was wide-ranging, both geographically and musically. He was invited to conduct in a variety of settings throughout the

Figure 5.1. Cecile and William Dawson. William Levi Dawson Papers. Reproduced by permission of the Milton L. Randolph Jr. Estate.

United States and in Spain, and frequently gave workshops and presentations at conferences for choral directors. He continued to be active as a composer and arranger but dedicated more energy to protecting the copyrights on his existing catalog than to creating new works.

Journeys Taken, Dreams Fulfilled

Tuskegee Institute granted Dawson a sabbatical in 1952–53; had his request been denied, he would have gone anyway.[2] Three years before his resignation, he was already beginning to break free from the constraints of his job.

Dawson's tour of six West African countries was the realization of a dream that began when, as a fourteen-year-old, he worked on the Tuskegee Institute farm alongside a student from Africa, and the two boys overcame their language barrier by singing to each other. Dawson wrote down the words of one of his friend's songs and discovered that their meaning was similar to the African American folk song *Nobody Knows the Trouble I've Seen*.[3] This musical encounter sparked a desire to visit the continent of his ancestors that finally came to fruition nearly forty years later. Dawson applied for a Fulbright Fellowship, but did not learn that his application had been successful until after he had returned from the trip, at which point he declined the fellowship. This may have been a blessing in disguise: he perceived that the Africans he met saw his interest in their music as more sincere because he hadn't been sent by a foundation, and may have shared more openly as a result.[4]

Dawson's visit to Africa was preceded by his first trip to Europe. His two weeks in England and France were themselves a musical feast, as he attended concerts by the Royal Philharmonic and the Vienna Philharmonic, a performance of *Samson et Dalila* at the Grand Opera House in Paris, Mass at Notre-Dame Cathedral (he wrote to Cecile, "I know what gothic architecture makes music sound like *now*! It is something that cannot be described in words!"), and a lecture-recital on Stravinsky by the famed composition teacher Nadia Boulanger, whom he met afterward.[5] In Paris he had lunch with Robert Salles, cellist of the Pascal Quartet, and the African American concert pianist Lois Towles. His cultural explorations also took him to a show of which he wrote saucily to Cecile: "I have been to the Folies-Bergere tonight. It is most spectacular. Something like the shows at Music Hall Radio City. Many women nude from the waist up and a fig leaf at the middle. Their breasts [were] not large but all of the same size etc."[6]

Dawson arrived in Dakar on December 1, 1952.[7] He spent two days there before setting out on a twelve-week itinerary that included two weeks in Sierra

Figure 5.2. Dawson recording balafon and bolon players in Africa. Tuskegee University Archives.

Leone, three in Liberia, three in the Gold Coast (now Ghana), one in Dahomey (now Benin), and three in Nigeria. He met government leaders, including Prime Minister Kwame Nkrumah of the Gold Coast and President William Tubman of Liberia, and musicians including the Sierra Leonean composer and scholar Nicholas G. J. Ballanta-Taylor. He brought a battery-powered tape recorder and a video camera with him, making dozens of field recordings now housed in the Dawson Collection at Emory University. His recordings—made in cities and villages, at homes and missions and colleges—record an impressive range of music and dancing by people ranging from professional musicians to three-year-old children. Characteristically, Dawson worked hard to record and learn as much as he possibly could during his stay.

In a letter to Cecile written not long after his arrival in Africa, Dawson wrote of his visit to Port Loko, east of Freetown, Sierra Leone, where he observed dancing and music-making that continued from afternoon until nearly midnight. After describing the dancing and singing in some detail, he turned to something that was to have a profound effect on his musical consciousness:

> Now as to the drums. I can not describe in words what it sounds like. Let me say this. The records that I have there at home with African music on them, sound like "child's play" when compared with what I heard at Port Loco [*sic*]. I was able to record this drumming and singing during the actual scene! The drummers like me so well that they waited until I went to the "rest house" where I slept to get my machine, and return to record them. The whole community remained too! It was about 10:30 P.M. when I made the recording.
>
> Darling, if I had to return this very moment, I would feel that my trip had been a huge success. I have learned so much in *two short weeks*. I'll know from now on, good drumming from that which is not so good. I am learning so much about the meaning this music, singing and drumming hold for their people.[8]

Dawson's experience of music in West Africa gave him a glimpse of the cultural richness and diversity from which his ancestors had been uprooted when they were sold into slavery. The enormity of the loss, symbolized by the *Negro Folk Symphony*'s recurring motive, became more vivid to him than ever. All of this led Dawson to bring the wealth of African music as he had come to understand it into his revision of the symphony, especially its newly explosive third movement.

While the impact of Dawson's time in Africa is obvious in the revisions he made to his symphony, it is more difficult to pinpoint related changes to his choral composition style, especially because he composed relatively few new works of any sort after 1950. The one distinctively different feature of his three choral pieces in the folk idiom from this period—*In His Care-O* (1961), *Zion's Walls* (1961), and *I Wan' to Be Ready* (1967)—is the unpredictability of their phrase lengths. Chapter 3 discusses the phrase structure of *In His Care-O* in some detail; the other two works likewise stray from the four-measure phrasing so ubiquitous in his earlier pieces (and in most arrangements of African American folk songs, broadly speaking). Given that the revisions Dawson made to his symphony also prominently include more expansive and irregular phrase lengths, it is plausible that this change was a direct consequence of the varied metrical structures he encountered in African music.

His discoveries in Africa may have influenced his 1955 essay for *Etude*, "Interpretation of the Religious Folk-Songs of the American Negro." In it, he emphasizes that "whether the singing of this music is alive or lifeless" is dependent upon its performers "keep[ing] in mind that music *per se* is invisible, and the notation or symbols we see on the staves and erroneously called music, are but the representation of sound. For this reason, we must first seek the *real* music, its emotional content and the message behind the symbols."[9] This idea was surely not unknown to Dawson before he heard music-making in Africa, but it is striking that he chose to emphasize it in this high-profile essay, since fidelity to the printed score was a pillar of his own classical training and of his teaching. The experience of sophisticated, skillfully performed, and brilliantly effective music-making in Africa that was unyoked to notation may have led him to recalibrate his priorities.

Less than four years after he returned from Africa, Dawson took his second life-changing trip, this one to Spain. The circumstances were very different: this time, he traveled at the behest of the U.S. government. During the Cold War, the U.S. State Department funded and oversaw various cultural outreach programs around the globe in an effort to sway public opinion toward democracy and away from communism. Charismatic artists of color were deployed as living proof that any American could rise to fame and success, regardless of race or background.[10] Dawson was one of several African American musicians, including Louis Armstrong and Lionel Hampton, whose tours of Spain the State Department supported in the mid-1950s. (The signing of the Pact of Madrid in 1953 had made Francisco Franco an important U.S. ally, and President Dwight D. Eisenhower hoped that the cultural ambassadors would help facilitate warm feelings in the Spanish people toward American military personnel newly stationed there.[11]) It was a difficult time for these Black artists to sing the praises of the United States. In 1955, the year before Dawson's visit to Spain, Rosa Parks was arrested for refusing to give up her seat on an Alabama bus, and fourteen-year-old Emmett Till was lynched in Mississippi.

Unlike Armstrong and Hampton, Dawson was not an emissary of jazz. Between July and September 1956, Dawson conducted Spanish choirs in programs consisting partly of African American folk songs arranged by himself and other Black composers, and partly of sacred works by the Spanish composer Tomàs Luis de Victoria (1548–1611). In a letter to Cecile from San Sebastián on July 23, 1956, Dawson wrote, "The trip is doing much to give the people of this country a different idea of the American Negro. Everybody thinks that all Negroes [are] 'Jazz hounds.' Everybody knows Louis Armstrong etc. The priests were reluctant about hav[ing] Negro songs in the Catholic Church, but when they learned what these songs express they were surprised but eager to hear them."[12]

Due to some scheduling difficulties, Dawson conducted three choirs in just four concerts during his ten weeks in Spain: the Orfeón Donostiarra (in San Sebastián, July 29 and 31), the Orfeó Lleidatà (Lerida, August 3), and the Coral Polifónica de la Empresa Nacional "Bazán" (Ferrol, September 20). The trip's organizer and Dawson's companion throughout the journey, Antonio Gonzales de la Peña, had originally intended for Dawson to conduct at least one additional choir, and the final concert was supposed to occur several weeks earlier. In his travel journal, Dawson repeatedly writes, "Still no date set for the concert!" The delay was not entirely a hardship; the relatively small amount of work he had to do during his stay in Spain left time for a great deal of sightseeing and socializing. He wrote to Cecile, "I am meeting all of the 'Greats' of Spain. Writers, painters, bankers, barons etc. Last night the Director of the Conservatory of Madrid, a great organist, came to my rehearsal and is coming to the concert Sunday. Madrid is about *200 miles* from San Sebastian."[13]

In his official report to the American Embassy in Madrid, Dawson describes spending hours in the company of various musicians and scholars, experiencing a musical and intellectual rapport that gave him great pleasure. In the course of one conversation he sang the religious folk songs of his ancestors for the director of the Escolania of Montserrat, Father P. Irineo, who then asked Dawson to send copies of his pieces so that he might use them with his choir. At the El Escorial monastery in Madrid, he heard the monks chant Mass, after which he and Father Samuel Rubio "spent several hours together in a discussion of Sixteenth Century polyphony and Negro 'spirituals,'" leading to yet another request for Dawson to send scores for Rubio's singers. Before they parted, Dawson wrote, "Padre Rubio autographed for me two of his most recent publications on Sixteenth Century polyphony which I very highly prize."[14] Dawson's entries in his travel journal are unrestrained in their delight: "What a life!" he wrote upon returning to his hotel at 2 a.m., having just listened to the Tuskegee Institute Choir's LP with some enthusiastic Spanish friends.[15]

The four concerts he conducted proved equally successful. The first, held on the 400th anniversary of the death of St. Ignatius of Loyola, was especially momentous. As he wrote home to Cecile, "It was something that I shall never forget. Thousands were turned away who could not get into the Sanctuary. Loud speakers were hung outside of the building. The Pope sent representatives from Rome! People came from all over Spain! The chorus sang wonderfully well. All adults. They rehearse five days a week throughout the year. This has been going on for years! The basses sound like Russian and the tenors sing high "C"s and sound like *Caruso*! A really wonderful chorus."[16]

Dawson missed Cecile during his ten weeks in Spain, but he seems otherwise to have had a nearly idyllic time. He received the respect that was his due as a leading American choral conductor, while also being treated with great personal warmth. Choirs rehearsed and sang with commitment; audiences were fascinated and enthusiastic. Those who had previously held narrow views of African American music readily acknowledged their error. At every turn, Dawson's eyes and ears were filled with the beauty and antiquity of Spanish culture, and he was surrounded by people as intellectually curious and beguiled by the arts as himself.

It may be thanks in part to his experience in Spain that Dawson built the rest of his career upon short-term engagements that allowed him to play the role of venerated guest. While conducting all-state choruses and leading educators' workshops in the United States did not always duplicate the high he experienced in Spain, he chose never again to subject himself to the quotidian hassles and indignities of a permanent academic post.

Itinerant Master

Home of the Fisk Jubilee Singers who had pioneered the concert performance of African American religious folk songs in the 1870s, Fisk was likely one of very few HBCUs that could have attracted Dawson after he resigned from Tuskegee. Hired for a one-year position, he conducted the Fisk University Choir (not the Jubilee Singers) in 1958–59, becoming that ensemble's first African American director.[17] Under Dawson's leadership the large choir performed in Fisk Memorial Chapel weekly. It also put on two impressive concerts. In the first, at Christmastime, the choir sang works by Dawson and John W. Work III, a Fisk faculty member, as well as compositions by George Frideric Handel, Gustav Holst, and Hector Berlioz. Louis Nicholas of the *Nashville Tennessean* reviewed the concert: "In its first full evening concert under the direction of Dr. William L. Dawson, long the director of the famous Tuskegee choir, the Fisk choir sang with notable beauty of tone, the clearest diction that I recall from this group, and with all the variety of shading that has characterized the group in the past, under its various excellent directors, and the virility and enthusiasm that it always possesses at its best."[18] It is noteworthy that Nicholas, a White critic, compared Dawson favorably to his White predecessors.

In April, for Fisk University's 30th Annual Festival of Music and Art, Dawson led an even more ambitious program. The first half included pieces by Black composers and arrangers (Work, Robert Nathaniel Dett, Hall Johnson, Gilbert Allen of the Wings over Jordan Choir, and Dawson himself) and Europeans (including several works by Tomàs Luis de Victoria). The second half consisted entirely of Samuel Coleridge-Taylor's *Hiawatha's Wedding Feast*, with participation by members of the Nashville Symphony Orchestra, Tennessee Agricultural & Industrial State University Band, and the Pearl High School Band. Dawson's nephew, Milton Randolph Jr., was tenor soloist. This concert spurred the reviewer from *The Nashville Banner* to write, "This year, under the direction of William L. Dawson, [the Fisk Choir] has made noticeable progress."[19] Nicholas reported that "the choir upheld its fine reputation nobly, and Dr. Dawson deserved the affectionate and enthusiastic applause showered upon him."[20]

A month earlier, Dawson had served as guest conductor for a concert by Nashville's Pearl High School Band, returning to his band roots. Again the programming was impressive, including Holst's popular *Second Suite in F for Military Band* and an arrangement of Tchaikovsky's *Romeo and Juliet*, as well as Dawson's own arrangement of a movement from Dett's *In the Bottoms* piano suite, titled *His Song*. An audio recording of the band rehearsing under Dawson gives a vivid sense of his infectious energy and exceptionally keen ear. He yells over the band's playing, sometimes about missed entrances, at other times to encourage the players ("Good! Good!"). At one point he stops the band to offer this wisdom: "When you're behind, you can't make it up by coming in fast." The ratio of playing to talking is high, however, reflecting Dawson's ability to communicate through gesture.[21]

Short-term, high-intensity engagements—working with a choir (or occasionally with a band or orchestra), giving lectures and demonstrations and workshops for fellow professionals—were a major feature of Dawson's career as an independent musician. A list in the Dawson Collection, "Highlights in the Career of William L. Dawson," which he compiled in the early 1980s, includes roughly a dozen each of lectures, clinics, and workshops, and some forty-plus appearances as guest conductor. These events took him across the United States, from Massachusetts to Hawaii, and to the US Virgin Islands and Quebec. Dawson's level of activity remained remarkably high well into his 80s; in just three months in the spring of 1984, for example, his professional activities ranged over seven states from coast to coast.[22]

Dawson frequently worked with very large groups. In January 1961 he conducted 420 singers in the All-Eastern Division Conference Chorus of the Music Educators National Conference in Washington, D.C. The correspondence leading up to this event reveals several aspects of Dawson's approach to his work as a guest conductor. First, he was unfailingly prompt, detailed, and polite in his communication with his fellow professionals, even when frustrated. Not long after his initial invitation in the summer of 1960, he was asked to provide his intended program as soon as possible. Having done so, he was then asked several times to make alterations based on criteria that shifted with each request ("excellent contemporary music by one of the great masters of choral writing"; "more ambitious, more standard").[23] Dawson stated in correspondence that he "wish[ed] that all that your committee has asked of me . . . could have been stated from the very beginning," but he complied, submitting in the end a program that differed substantially from his first version.[24]

A second evident feature of Dawson's approach is that he was careful to define the parameters of his responsibility. Violet Johnson, who handled most of the communication in the lead-up to this event, asked him to write a letter for distribution beforehand "to encourage and help impress on students the fact that the music should be all learned and memorized before coming to Washington, D.C., and to the teachers to help them, in a nice way, to share more in the responsibility of teaching the students."[25] As an example, she provided a lengthy and genial letter written by his predecessor the prior year. Dawson responded, "I feel that the responsibility of encouraging the students to learn and memorize their parts etc. [is] not something that I should attempt. I am sure your organization would ask the supervisors, teachers of music and others to encourage the students to do their very best to prepare themselves for such an occasion as an All-Eastern program."[26] The letter that Dawson did ultimately write to the choir members was encouraging, but brief and businesslike. By emphasizing the significance of the event as the motivation for the students to learn their parts, he avoided being blamed if they were to arrive underprepared. As an African American in a field dominated by Whites, he was wise to minimize the likelihood that his authority and competence would be questioned.

A dramatic demonstration of Dawson's willingness to hold others to account for their preparation came in March 1965, when he went to Texas Southern University for events that included a massed high school choir. Choral director Clyde Owen Jackson recounts:

> When Dawson agreed to come, the understanding was that the choirs would be "taught the notes" of the songs (Dawson arrangements) by their directors before they left for Houston. He would then rehearse them all together that afternoon in preparation for the evening concert. He began working with these high school students. My heart sank. I knew what was coming. We (the TSU faculty) and the high school choir directors were sitting in the auditorium seats while he worked with the choirs on stage. He turned to the directors sitting in the audience and said, "Your students don't know this music." He canceled the concert![27]

Jackson tells this story as an example of Dawson being "brutally frank." One could also read it as exemplifying Dawson's willingness to be frankly brutal: this episode must have been very disappointing for the students. Again, race was a factor in his actions, but this time the circumstances and the message were different. Texas public schools were still largely segregated in 1965, and the high school choirs participating in this event came from "colored" schools. By calling out the choir directors' failure to adequately prepare their students, and by refusing to participate in producing a mediocre concert, Dawson sent a powerful message to every educator present: do not sell these young people short. Dawson's display of self-respect and high standards doubtless made a lasting impression on all present, teachers and students alike.

His work with fellow choral directors constituted almost as significant a component of his post-Tuskegee career as did his work with young singers. Already in 1956, when he received the honorary doctorate from Tuskegee, the citation noted that he was often "called upon by public school systems in the East to give demonstrations in the teaching of music to teachers of music. It is not to be wondered that in your profession you are known as [a] 'musicians' musician.'"[28] Over the following three decades of his career, he was invited to give numerous workshops and demonstrations for choral directors around the country, speaking to large audiences, with many repeat engagements.

When educating his fellow educators, Dawson preferred to assemble choral directors into a chorus and work with them that way, rather than having them passively observe as he worked with a "demonstration choir." He conducted a directors' chorus in Rochester, New York, as early as 1946, and continued to accept such invitations and to actively promote this method as late as 1986, when he conducted at the state convention of the American Choral Directors Association (ACDA) in Mississippi. He also led a number of score-reading sessions on behalf of various publishers and in 1979 and 1980 partnered with composer and choral director John Haberlen in a series of ten successful choral workshops to promote their publications with Neil A. Kjos Music Company. In an interview, Haberlen said that during their trips together Dawson became a "friend and mentor" who took pleasure in sharing his knowledge about African American history and music with his White touring companion. Haberlen described Dawson as a "virile" conductor who led choirs powerfully with his body, his strong singing and speaking voice, and his remarkable knowledge and musical memory.[29]

Dawson was frequently invited to give lectures on topics including the history and performance of African American religious folk songs, Black contributions to classical music, his own choral works and *Negro Folk Symphony*, and techniques of arranging for male voices. In the Dawson Collection at Emory University, his undated notes for a lecture illuminate his values as a conductor. He spends much of the lecture emphasizing that a musical leader needs "absolute confidence in his general ability and profound knowledge of the particular subject being handled."

Figure 5.3. Dawson conducting the Germantown Friends High School Chorus, 1981. Leandre Jackson, photographer. William Levi Dawson Papers, series 8, box 52, folder 34. Reproduced by permission of the Milton L. Randolph Jr. Estate.

He details the many areas in which a director must be well versed (harmony, musical form, counterpoint, vocal anatomy, music history, details of each score being performed) and skilled (keyboard facility, rhythmic sense, conducting, "a refined ear"). Dawson acknowledges that some in his audience may find this long list of requirements discouraging, and offers as encouragement that "many excellent singing groups have been developed by conductors deficient in one or more of these necessities." However, he insists that conductors must "strive to know as much as possible," as the limits of their musical knowledge define the limits of what they can think to ask of a choir. He also notes that "to be a teacher means to be an example"—a responsibility that he fully embraced.[30]

Dawson served as an authority and role model for many in the choral conducting world, with a particularly strong impact on his younger Black colleagues. He was an active member of the ACDA, and one of its few members of color. At the 1975 national convention in St. Louis, he was recognized by the ACDA "for his pioneering leadership, inspiration, and service."[31] When a symposium was convened by Eugene Thamon Simpson in September 1979, leading to the creation of the ACDA Committee on Ethnic Music and Minority Concerns (today known as the Diversity Initiatives Committee), one of its recommendations was that every national and division convention should include "a minority 'star' session." Dawson was the first star recommended, for the 1981 national convention.[32] This did not come to fruition, but he did lead sessions at regional conventions, including the Western Division in 1983, the Southern Division in 1984, and the Northwest Division in 1986.

Dawson was a widely admired figure in the White-dominated field of choral music. Although he was a warm person whose support and friendship were invaluable to many younger choir directors, he maintained a professional persona that was formal, authoritative, and always in control. This image helped Dawson take advantage of the respect to which his masculinity gave him access as a straight, cisgender man. The high regard in which he was held did not neutralize the effect of structural racism on the second half of his career: despite his fame and status in the field, no predominantly White institution sought him as a faculty member after he left Tuskegee in his mid-50s.

Honors and awards rolled in during these decades, however. In 1963 he received an Alumni Achievement Award from the University of Missouri at Kansas City, which had absorbed the Horner Institute of Fine Arts (from which he had graduated in 1925). Dawson was awarded honorary doctorates from Lincoln University in 1978 and, poignantly, from Ithaca College in 1982—six decades after he had given up on Pat Conroy's bandmaster program there. He was recognized by his home state: he was inducted into the Alabama Arts Hall of Fame in 1975 and into the Alabama Music Hall of Fame in 1989, and he received the Governor's Arts Award in 1986. Cities including Birmingham, Atlanta, Baltimore, and Philadelphia celebrated Dawson with keys, citations, and declarations of "William L. Dawson Day." He was initiated to honorary membership in the men's music fraternity Phi Mu Alpha in 1977. He was honored by institutions ranging from the Abyssinian Baptist Church of New York City (1969) to the Eva Jessye Afro-American Collection at the University of Michigan (1981) to the performance rights organization SESAC (Paul Heinecke Citation of Merit, 1983). He received official recognition from Tuskegee (which became Tuskegee University in 1985) several times in addition to the honorary doctorate in 1956, receiving the Philadelphia Alumni Chapter Award in 1971, the Tuskegee Alumni Merit Award in 1983, and the Board of Trustees Distinguished Service Award in 1989.

The Creative Artists' Workshop was a nonprofit organization founded in the mid-1970s by composer and flutist Leslie Burrs to create new opportunities for African American artists. Burrs, with the help of the scholar (and friend of Dawson) James Spady, arranged a remarkable set of events in November 1981 to promote, document, and celebrate Dawson's accomplishments. Cecile Dawson, whose health was beginning to decline, was able to accompany her husband to Philadelphia for the weekend. Sylvia Olden Lee, famed vocal coach and collaborative pianist on the Curtis Institute of Music faculty, hosted a welcoming reception at Curtis. On November 20, Dawson began the day with a lecture-demonstration at the Germantown Friends School, hearing the choir sing three of his folk song arrangements and then working with the young singers. Burrs wrote:

> One young man was designated to sing the solo section. There he stood, in front of all his peers and this international composer whose work he was about to perform. His voice was at that tender age when it couldn't decide if it should sound like a man or a boy, so after every few notes it would crack. Yet he still gave it his all. His solo proved to be a fine rendition of that *Balm In Gilead*. Mr. Dawson was very proud of that young man's performance and made it known. It was a memorable and heartwarming experience.[33]

Dawson's day continued with a reception at Philadelphia City Hall, where he received a citation from Mayor Bill Green.

In the evening, Dawson conducted a concert of his own works, sung by the Mendelssohn Singers and guest soloist John R. Russell. The venue was the Academy of Music, where the Tuskegee Institute Choir had sung under Dawson nearly fifty years earlier, and where the *Negro Folk Symphony* had its premiere in 1934. The program included many of his most popular Tuskegee-era works, including *Ain'a That Good News* and *Ezekiel Saw de Wheel*, but also included newer compositions such as *Zion's Walls* and *In His Care-O*. Three of the program's thirteen pieces by Dawson lay outside of the African American folk song genre with which he was most associated: *Out in the Fields*, *The Rugged Yank*, and *Before the Sun Goes Down*. The first of these, composed in memory of Dawson's first wife, had first been published in 1929; the last, a lovely setting of a poem by Edith Sanford Tillotson to the tune of "Londonderry Air," was his last published work (1978). The concert, performed to an enthusiastic full house, truly represented a culmination of Dawson's career. In a gesture that reflected his gratitude for the event, Dawson donated his $1,300 conductor's fee to the Creative Artists' Workshop.

James Spady's efforts to celebrate and commemorate Dawson's achievements that weekend included a longer-lasting component. He compiled and edited a collection of writings by and about Dawson, titled *William L. Dawson: A UMUM Tribute and a Marvelous Journey*, which was distributed after the event to a number of institutions including Tuskegee University, Lincoln University, New York's

Schomburg Library, and the Free Library of Philadelphia. The booklet includes Dawson's 1955 *Etude* article, "Interpretation of the Religious Folk-Songs of the American Negro"; writings (both old and new) about Dawson and his music by Roy Wilkins, Abbie Mitchell, Mark Perry, Shirley Graham Du Bois, Eileen Southern, Leopold Stokowski, Bernice Johnson Reagon, and others; a list of works, discography, and bibliography; and a lengthy biographical essay by Spady. This last item, aside from a few inaccuracies, provides remarkable details and insights regarding the first thirty-five years of Dawson's life and his early career.[34] The booklet, not easy to come by today, for four decades constituted the closest thing to a book about Dawson, alongside the handful of doctoral dissertations listed in the Bibliography.

Managing a Legacy

Dawson continued composing and arranging into his 80s, but his pace of creation slowed considerably after he left Tuskegee's faculty. Nonetheless, his identity and legacy as a composer remained deeply important to him, and he dedicated significant attention and resources to the preservation and protection of that legacy.

After encountering racist discrimination from various music publishers in the 1920s and '30s Dawson had, with assistance from Cecile, spent decades handling every element of printing and selling his music. In the 1960s, he reached out again to the publishing industry. In 1967, Dawson entered into an arrangement with the Neil A. Kjos Music Company, retaining all his copyrights but rendering Kjos the sole distributor of his vocal works. Dawson's correspondence with the company's owner attests to a warm relationship, and the company's representatives showed the composer great respect. The terms of the business relationship were favorable, with Dawson receiving 60% of net sales. In some years, his royalties from Kjos reached five digits, constituting a substantial proportion of the household income.[35]

Around the same time, in 1965, Dawson entered into an arrangement with Pennsylvania's Shawnee Press, making it the sole selling agent of his *Negro Folk Symphony*. Although Shawnee helped with the rental and distribution of the score, Dawson retained his copyright and total control over the work itself. Thus, when Tilford Brooks included short excerpts of the *Negro Folk Symphony* in *America's Black Musical Heritage* (Englewood Cliffs, NJ: Prentice-Hall, 1984) with the indication that they were used with the permission of Shawnee Press, the composer reacted angrily, writing to an attorney and contemplating a lawsuit. The attorney persuaded Dawson not to pursue legal action against Brooks, given that the infringement was minor, the book's discussion of Dawson was positive, and the compensation he could expect in the event of a favorable court decision would not be worth the time and expense required to bring the suit.[36]

Dawson's unhappiness went beyond the issue of permission. In a letter to a friend, he tellingly complained that the excerpts Brooks had included contained errors and omissions that would lead readers to "question his . . . ability to utilize properly the instruments at his disposal etc."[37] The *Negro Folk Symphony* was the result of the composer's hard-won education, years of compositional labor, and unflagging determination despite the odds against the work ever being performed, let alone winning acclaim. As Dawson's only large-scale orchestral work, it was uniquely central to his reputation as a composer, and he was on the alert for any representation of it—even positive—that could call his competence into question.

Dawson poured time and money into both promoting and protecting the *Negro Folk Symphony* in the 1960s and '70s. He corresponded extensively with orchestras around the country, urging them to consider programming the work. Orchestras that rented the score and parts were often directed to return them not to Shawnee Press but to Dawson himself so that he could remove any markings made by the conductor or players. He also paid to have the score's three movements individually bound so that they could be sent out separately. In short, after the arrangement with Shawnee was made in 1963, Dawson still maintained responsibility for the *Negro Folk Symphony* score.

His concern for his magnum opus went beyond promoting and protecting the score. In a 1976 newspaper article, Richard Friedman describes the scene:

The man picked up a razor blade, held it for a moment between the thumb and forefinger of his right hand, and then began gently scratching the surface of a sheet of music.

With the patience and skill of a shoemaker—which he had been trained to be more than 50 years ago—the 76-year-old black man worked his brown hands deftly across the page.

Alone, at a wooden table in the library of the Birmingham Symphony, Tuskegee conductor and composer William Dawson worked quietly, making minor changes in his "Negro Folk Symphony," which he will conduct tonight at the Civic Center.

He scratched the surface some more, slowly lifting several inked notes from tiny spaces they occupied, until the small black impressions disappeared. Then, he began drawing new notes in their places.

Dawson, as he explained, was making some "alterations" in his symphony, before he and the orchestra would begin rehearsing a few minutes later. The changes he made he could not put in words, he said, they were just something he had heard.[38]

Friedman was not the first White writer to emphasize the contrast between the kind of manual labor a White reader might expect a Black man to do and the work of composing a symphony. This tendency dated back at least to 1934, when an Associated Press article on the symphony's triumphant premiere described Dawson as a "one-time boot-black."[39] The passage by Friedman is notable for lingering so avidly on "brown hands" laboring with a razor blade. In addition to shedding light on the attitudes that Dawson was still facing in the 1970s, this passage also shows his ongoing, intimate engagement with his symphony's score.

As might be expected, these continuing alterations took their toll on the rental score and parts. In 1978, Frederic Johnson of Diablo Valley College reacted strongly, writing to Shawnee Press that the rental materials were "in such poor condition as to be unreadable." In a fit of pique he enclosed a mock invoice for the cost of an eraser, four hours of "erasure," and a bottle of tranquilizer pills. A representative from Shawnee replied angrily that the work had been "performed widely" from the score and parts in question, and that "Mr. Ormandy had no problem [with them], nor did Mr. Stokowski," prompting Johnson to retort that "their librarians and other paid staff handle these details. I, and hundreds of other provincial conductors, don't enjoy that luxury." The correspondence concluded with Johnson noting that unless the publisher acted, "Conductors will continue to buy clean, new parts and scores to Beethoven, Brahms, et al [*sic*], because it is easier. Works like the one in question will continue to have one more strike against receiving extensive hearings."[40]

Johnson made an astute point. Unfortunately, a list of royalty payments paid to Dawson by Shawnee Press between 1965 and 1981 totaling only $424.50 (approximately $30 per year) may help to explain why the press made no move to print a new edition.[41] After the rise of the Black Lives Matter movement and the protests ignited by the 2020 murder of George Floyd led many American symphony orchestras to develop an interest in diverse programming, G. Schirmer (which through a series of acquisitions in the intervening years had become the symphony's rental agency) initiated the creation of a new performing edition of the *Negro Folk Symphony*, which became available in 2023.

Dawson's symphony was unquestionably precious to him, but he was equally vigilant and forceful in protecting his choral works from copyright infringement. Repeatedly over the years, distinctive artistic elements of his folk song settings were assumed by others to be in the public domain, leading to reprintings and more subtle borrowings without permission or acknowledgment. While appropriate financial compensation was a consideration, no less important to Dawson was his stature as a composer of original works. That many of these were arrangements of folk songs did not lessen their uniqueness, nor diminish his creativity and artistry.

A letter Dawson wrote to Robert W. Thygerson in 1978 makes his perspective on infringement very clear. Thygerson had published an arrangement of *Ain-A That Good News* that too closely resembled Dawson's own. Dawson had written to request that the younger composer identify his sources for the folk song. Thygerson's response prompted this in return:

> The three melodies to which you refer as your source are, to say the least, primitive and unsophisticated. They are traditional in the true sense of the word "traditional." Also, you will see the difference between a traditional melody and one that is not.
>
> What you saw in John Work's book is not what you see in "Ain'-A That Good News!" by Dawson. It is evident that the melody by Dawson is consciously shaped and constructed so as to obtain an original musical composition that has an aesthetic quality.
>
> No one would deny that the three primitive or unsophisticated tunes in John Work's book are traditional; but, "Ain'-A That Good News!" *by Dawson* is what *you* used. Not only did you use the exact title but also the exact melody, exact rhythmics, and structural features that had been arrived at creatively![42]

None of Dawson's choral arrangements of folk songs could be considered "primitive and unsophisticated"; each was original, creative, and carefully constructed for aesthetic effect. He was deeply offended when his compositions were appropriated as if they were folk songs. At the same time, it is crucial to note that his arrangements, conducting, teaching, and speaking about the folk songs of his ancestors invariably showed his deep respect for them. His letter to Thygerson represents a vanishingly rare instance of him using words like "primitive and unsophisticated" to describe the songs, and he does so here only to drive home his point about the difference between the original forms and his own creative work.

John B. Haberlen wrote in 1983, "Melodic, rhythmic, and harmonic motives from Dawson's arrangement of *There Is a Balm in Gilead* have appeared without authorization or permission, as the creation of other arrangers in no less than 12 hymnals and sacred song collections."[43] That particular song was especially prone to infringement, but because of Dawson's unique title (the folk song was previously known as *Balm in Gilead*) and distinctive meter changes, infringements could be identified. Several pages of handwritten notes in the Dawson Collection at Emory University show the composer perusing hymnals for unauthorized "Balms." Either directly or through his lawyer, M. William Krasilovsky, Dawson routinely reached out to composers and publishers, calling infringements to their attention and enclosing a copy of a public domain version so that they could quickly discern the difference. These efforts were usually successful without need for litigation;

the offending parties canceled publication, made changes, or offered compensation. (Dawson was only satisfied by the first of these options.)

Unfortunately the composer's final copyright battle became a morass that consumed vast sums of money during the last years of his life.[44] In 1986, against the advice of Krasilovsky, Dawson filed suit against Gilbert M. Martin and Hinshaw Music for Martin's 1981 arrangement titled *Ezekiel Saw the Wheel*.[45] Martin claimed that he was unfamiliar with Dawson's 1942 publication, and that his only reference had been the simple harmonization of the song found in John W. Work's 1940 collection, *American Negro Folk Songs*. Dawson noted that Martin's arrangement resembled his own in several ways, notably in its inclusion of a distinctive circling section that included the repetition of the phrase "wheel in a wheel." Confident that his copyright had been infringed, he demanded that Hinshaw cease publication of Martin's arrangement.

At a certain point in the proceedings, Dawson's legal representatives urged him to drop the case, noting that it would be difficult to prove that Martin had known and copied Dawson's *Ezekiel Saw de Wheel*, and that he would inevitably lose money even if he won the suit. However, Hinshaw Music refused to settle unless they were reimbursed for the hefty legal expenses they had already incurred, a condition that essentially forced Dawson to press on. The case continued until 1988, costing Dawson tens of thousands of dollars that he struggled to pay. The judge ultimately found in favor of Hinshaw because, as law scholar Charles Cronin explains, "Dawson had not presented recordings of performances of the two arrangements. The district court found that, as an ordinary lay observer, with nothing before him other than the sheet music, he could not determine that the two works were substantially similar." On appeal, the Fourth Circuit disagreed with the decision, noting that "[o]nly a reckless indifference to common sense would lead a court to embrace a doctrine that requires a copyright case to turn on the opinion of someone who is ignorant of the relevant differences and similarities between two works." The audience for the two arrangements was not the "ordinary lay listener" who could make neither heads nor tails of sheet music, but choral directors who most certainly could. Establishing an important precedent for future cases, this vindication arrived in April 1990, four weeks after Dawson's death.[46]

Ceremonies and Farewells

On September 24, 1989, two days before his ninetieth birthday, Tuskegee held a ceremonious celebration for William Dawson in the University Chapel. The music included an organ prelude performed by Roy Edward Hicks, congregational singing of several hymns, and abundant choral music by Dawson. The Tuskegee University Choir performed, as did the newly formed Dawson Alumni Choir (which continues to the present day), both directed by Clyde Owen Jackson. Video of the event shows Dawson sitting impassively through most of the proceedings, showing little response to the performances, formal speeches, and accolades. He reacted most warmly to the unscripted words of Tuskegee Institute Choir alumni such as Laura McCray, who concluded her brief remarks, "God bless you as you continue my dear. I love you."[47]

At two points Dawson participated actively in the event. He conducted the alumni in a performance of *Ain'-A That Good News*. He had twice rehearsed this group in preparation, as alumna Virginia Campbell-Hawkins later described:

> When he walked in, it was just like we remembered him years ago. He had to shake everybody's hand. Then he said, "Now, let's get down to business."
>
> And did we ever get down to business. During rehearsal, he got after us, just the way he had always done, about pronouncing the words. It was like old times. Loads of people had come back for the birthday celebration.[48]

In the video recording of the performance, Dawson conducts economically, with flexible pacing and a light, relaxed energy. The choir's rhythm is precise, with clear diction and distinct dynamics. Most notable is the choir's obvious confidence and comfort. The audience begins to applaud wildly even before the last note is cut off, and the choir joins in the applause as soon as they finish singing. McCray rushes from the choir to give Dawson a hug, which he happily returns.

Several speeches later, the guest of honor is invited to speak. He takes less than two minutes.

> Thank you, ladies and gentlemen, and everyone that's in this house. I've got to say something that is a very old story, but this is the only thing I can think of that just fit this occasion. During the First World War, they drafted a little fellow who couldn't read nor write. And they say, "We're gonna put you in the army."
>
> And he looked at 'em peculiarly and he says, "For what?"
>
> They said, "We're gonna put you in the army, we're gonna give you 30 dollars a month, we're gonna give you a free uniform, and we want you to fight the Kuzzah [i.e., Kaiser]."
>
> He said, "Where dat Kuzzah been all this time, he ain't started this war?"
>
> So I wonder, where has all this been all this time that you haven't done this to me?
>
> I am speechless, but I am most grateful to you because this doesn't happen every day and I appreciate it greatly. There's a whole lot of things I could say, but we've been here long enough [audience laughter] and I'm not gonna say any more but just thank you from the bottom of my heart and I hope this is the beginning for me to do something better. Thank you very, very much.[49]

It is remarkable that a man renowned at Tuskegee for his seriousness and intensity should dedicate so much of what was to be his last public speech to a joke. The choice enabled him both to mitigate some of the event's pomp and to gently express his ambivalence about the institution honoring him. His great achievements as a composer, choral director, and educator had been launched by his Tuskegee education, and his illustrious twenty-five-year career on the faculty had amply demonstrated his loyalty and dedication to the Institute. At the same time, he remembered the frustration he had encountered during his tenure and always felt a twinge when the institution celebrated him and his accomplishments after the fact.

One last point from this speech bears emphasis. Near the end of a long, generous life full of groundbreaking work, Dawson still spoke of "do[ing] something better." As much as he expected from those around him, he never stopped demanding even more from himself.

On May 2, 1990, William Levi Dawson passed in a Montgomery hospital. For several years he had lovingly cared for Cecile, whose health had deteriorated slowly as a result of complications from diabetes. When no longer able to care for her in their home, he had driven daily from Tuskegee to Montgomery to visit her in the hospital and assisted living facility. She passed on Valentine's Day, 1993.

Dawson's funeral, held in the Tuskegee Chapel, was even more lavishly musical than his ninetieth birthday celebration had been. It included an organ prelude, congregational singing of *Lift Ev'ry Voice and Sing*, and three pieces played by the Tuskegee University Concert Band under Warren L. Duncan II. Music by Dawson permeated the proceedings, with several HBCU choirs contributing performances: Florida A&M University Choir (directed by Augustus Pearson Jr.), Auburn University Choir (Thomas Smith), Spelman College Choir (Norma Raybon), and the Morehouse College Glee Club (Harding Epps). The Tuskegee University Choir and the Dawson Alumni Choir performed, directed again by Clyde Owen Jackson.

Milton L. Randolph Jr., the son of Dawson's sister Odessa, was Dawson's heir. After determining that the archives at Tuskegee University were not well equipped to handle such a large amount of material, Randolph donated the William Levi Dawson Papers to the Stuart A. Rose Manuscript, Archives, and Rare Book Library at Emory University. The collection is a treasure trove for researchers. A symposium held at Emory in March 2005, "In Celebration of William L. Dawson: An Exploration of African-American Music and Identity at the Dawn of the 21st Century," featured presentations by Randolph and a dazzling array of scholars and musicians including Geri Allen, Rae Linda Brown, Marva Griffin Carter, Anthony Davis, Tania León, Olly Wilson, and many more.[50]

Since Randolph's passing in 2015, his daughter Jennifer Randolph has managed the Dawson estate. She visited him and Cecile in Alabama as a child, and remembers her great-uncle vividly as an impeccable dresser and a terrifyingly distracted driver. When he learned that she was going to study abroad in France, he insisted on speaking to her only in French; later, when she was bound for Italy during college, he would converse only in Italian. They didn't speak often by phone, but Dawson was always able to pick up where their last conversation left off. Randolph says he was an impressive, highly respected family member.[51]

A Gift

Among those contributing to the booklet compiled for the Creative Artists' Workshop tribute to Dawson in 1981 was Bernice Johnson Reagon, a prolific activist-scholar-musician who had encountered him decades earlier when she was a student at Spelman College. A renowned champion of African American history, culture, and liberation since the early 1960s, her testimonial speaks to the impact of his words and example on so many people, especially young Black people, whose lives he touched.

> And then one day, during weekly convocation in Sisters Chapel, he was there on our stage and he gave me a gift that I have used many times since. We loved hearing his early story about growing up poor, and becoming famous, and we laughed at his current experiences at trying to get a predominantly white choir to execute some of his compositions studded with their multiple rhythms. However, the riveting statement that touched me most was his struggle to become a musician; he needed a place to study; the conservatory in question would not accept Blacks as students; with persistent negotiations he extracted an agreement to be taught separately at night. He told us it was the same theory, harmony, and composition, maybe better, because of the teacher/pupil ratio of one to one. What stuck with me was that when Dawson came to be who he could become, he found that there was no way, no door, no path; he just proceeded to make one—it was the "way out of no way" that I have carried. It made me a partner in my life with my mother who, following her mother, had done it many times. And so, in 1969, armed with a fellowship to do my doctoral research and wanting to study oral history as a way to focus on the culture legacy of my people—when I found there was no program—no way—I saw it only as a signal of the nature of the task ahead and moved on, negotiating a way to acquire the skills I needed to be more of who I felt I could be.
>
> Thank you Professor Dawson, I'm still trying.[52]

Figure 5.4. Dawson, 1989. Property of the author.

NOTES

Preface

1. Nell Irvin Painter, "Opinion: Why 'White' Should Be Capitalized, Too," *The Washington Post*, July 22, 2020, https://www.washingtonpost.com/opinions/2020/07/22/why-white-should-be-capitalized/.

Introduction

1. Nikole Hannah-Jones, press release, July 6, 2021, https://www.naacpldf.org/wp-content/uploads/NHJ-Statement-CBS-7.6.21-FINAL-8-am.pdf.

2. Video of 24th Annual William Levi Dawson Lecture by Horace Maxile, April 12, 2015, https://www.youtube.com/watch?v=SEyQtpUqThk.

3. Smith, *William Grant Still*; Rae Linda Brown, *The Heart of a Woman*; Malone, *William Levi Dawson*.

4. Gwynne Kuhner Brown, "Whatever Happened to William Dawson's *Negro Folk Symphony*?" *Journal of the Society for American Music* 6, no. 4 (November 2012): 433–56.

5. See Gwynne Kuhner Brown, "Gender in the Life."

Chapter 1. Early Life

1. Gary Sprayberry, "Anniston," http://encyclopediaofalabama.org/article/h-1464; Patricia Hoskins Morton, "Calhoun County," http://encyclopediaofalabama.org/article/h-1198; Malone, *William Levi Dawson*, 8.

2. William Levi Dawson (1886–1970), who served in the House of Representatives for many years, was the composer's first cousin.

3. Unless otherwise noted, biographical details come from Dawson's typed autobiographical notes from around 1946 and from his handwritten notes from around 1973. William Levi Dawson Papers, series 6, box 37, folder 3.

4. Damon Adams, "Award-winning Conductor Still Strives for Perfection," *Anniston Star*, January 10, 1987, William Levi Dawson Papers, series 9, box 69.

5. Autobiographical notes, William Levi Dawson Papers, series 6, box 37, folder 3.

6. Malone, *William Levi Dawson*, 9.

7. Ibid.

8. Ibid., 10.

9. Buckner, "Rediscovering Major N. Clark Smith," 38.

10. Du Bois, *The Souls of Black Folk*, 44.

11. Ibid., 40.

12. Dawson, audio recording of interview, Philadelphia, October 1979, William Levi Dawson Papers, series 11.

13. Wyatt, "Composers Corner," 7.

14. The architect Robert Robinson Taylor (1868–1942), who designed several buildings on the Tuskegee campus, graduated from MIT in 1892. Monroe Nathan Work (1866–1945) earned a master of arts degree in sociology from the University of Chicago in 1903.

15. Dawson interview, October 1979.

16. *Tuskegee Normal and Industrial Institute Bulletin* 9, no. 2 (1915): 38; quoted in McMillan, "The Choral Music," 80.

17. Jennie C. Lee (1866–1956) served as Tuskegee's second choir director from 1903 to 1928.

18. Travel Diaries, 1918–21, William Levi Dawson Papers, series 6, box 41.

19. Wallace, "The Choral Tradition," 103.

20. Malone, *William Levi Dawson*, 25.

21. Hood, "William Levi Dawson and His Music," 9.

22. William and Cecile Dawson, interview by James Standifer. The manuscript of Dawson's *Romance for Violin*, dated March 3, 1922, can be found in William Levi Dawson Papers, series 2, box 18, folder 1.

23. Malone, *William Levi Dawson*, 26–27.

24. Chris Outwin, "William Dawson—Ithaca at Last," unnamed newspaper article, n.d., William Levi Dawson Papers, series 9, box 67.

25. Unlabeled 1926 newspaper clipping, William Levi Dawson Papers, series 6, box 41, folder 9.

26. William and Cecile Dawson, interview by James Standifer.

27. Graham defines and examines the commercial spiritual as a category in *Spirituals and the Birth of a Black Entertainment Industry*, chapter 6.

28. Malone, *William Levi Dawson*, 28.

29. Mike Land, "Disharmony: Composer Overcomes Prejudices on Way to Success," *Alabama Journal*, January 2, 1987, William Levi Dawson Papers, series 9, box 69, folder 3. In 1923, Dawson received a Public School Music Certificate from Horner; it is unclear whether his studies for this certificate overlapped with those leading to his bachelor of music degree in 1925, nor whether there was some impetus from Lincoln High School for him to receive certification. The stories that Dawson and others told about Horner seem to refer exclusively to his studies leading to the BM in music theory.

30. Citron, "Gender, Professionalism and the Musical Canon," 105.

31. Dawson to Carl Busch, December 11, 1934; letter of recommendation by Busch, June 1926, William Levi Dawson Papers, series 1.

32. Wilkins, *The Autobiography of Roy Wilkins*, 69.

33. James Felton, "No 'Honky Tonk Stuff' for This Old Jazzman," *Philadelphia Bulletin*, October 7, 1979, William Levi Dawson Papers, series 9, box 69, folder 2.

34. Dawson to H. O. Cook, September 7, 1925, William Levi Dawson Papers, series 1.

35. Carl Busch to William Dawson, January 1925, William Levi Dawson Papers, series 1.

36. Wyatt, "Composers Corner," 6.

37. Chet Fuller, "Black Composer Dawson's Works Honored," *Atlanta Constitution*, January 27, 1974, William Levi Dawson Papers, series 9, box 69, folder 2.

38. Tick, *Ruth Crawford Seeger*, 35.

39. Dawson to Regina Hall, December 11, 1934, William Levi Dawson Papers, series 1.

40. Adams, "Award-winning Conductor Still Strives for Perfection."

41. Dawson to John Lasher, draft, n.d. (ca. 1984), William Levi Dawson Papers, series 6, box 38, folder 2.

42. Rae Linda Brown, "William Grant Still," 76.

43. Hood, "William Levi Dawson and His Music," 13.

44. "A Tuskegee Symphony: Stokowski to Present Dawson's Pioneer Work on Negro Themes," *New York Times*, November 18, 1934.

45. Malone, *William Levi Dawson*, 33.

46. Samantha Ege's "Composing a Symphonist" provides a wonderful account of the community of women that surrounded Price in Chicago.

47. Rae Linda Brown, *The Heart of a Woman*, 108–9.

48. *Howard University Bison, 1924*, https://dh.howard.edu/cgi/viewcontent.cgi?article =1103&context=bison_yearbooks.

49. Unlabeled newspaper clipping, William Levi Dawson Papers, series 7, box 42, folder 12.

50. "A History of the Lyceum Series," http://web.nccu.edu/shepardlibrary/pdfs/centennial/ LyceumSeries.pdf.

51. Malone, *William Levi Dawson*, 35.

52. Mike Land, "Disharmony."

53. Charles Landsidle to Dawson, September 9, 1930, William Levi Dawson Papers, series 1.

54. Contract with Church of the Good Shepherd, Chicago, September 18, 1929, William Levi Dawson Papers, series 1.

55. "Negro Bandmaster Leads 35th Entry in Contest," unlabeled 1929 newspaper clipping. Tuskegee University Archives, Box 027.002.

56. Charles L. Yoder to Dawson, May 2, 1928, William Levi Dawson Papers, series 1.

57. Voter registration certificate, April 10, 1928, William Levi Dawson Papers, series 7, box 42, folder 15.

58. McMillan, 79.

59. Spady, "Eye Awadura Ma Efree Owura William L. Dawson maa okoo Kumasi/ Africa," in *William L. Dawson*, ed. Spady, 39.

Chapter 2. Tuskegee

1. R. Nathaniel Dett, "As the Negro School Sings," *Southern Workman* 56 (July 1927), 304–5; in *The R. Nathaniel Dett Reader*, ed. Jon Michael Spencer, 69.

2. Several letters testify to this friendship. Among the most interesting is one from January 8, 1925, in which Dett apologizes profusely to Dawson for the painful loss of some original manuscripts the young man had sent, William Levi Dawson Papers, series 1.

3. Schenbeck provides a riveting account of Dett's conflicts with the White leadership of Hampton Institute in chapter 4 of *Racial Uplift and American Music*. See also chapter 2 of Spencer, *The New Negroes and Their Music*.

4. Kaylina Madison Crawley, "John Wesley Work III: Arranger, Preserver, and Historian of African American Traditional Music" (PhD diss., University of Kentucky, 2021), 32–39.

5. Shortly after the premiere of the *Negro Folk Symphony*, Childers wrote to congratulate Dawson, and to inquire whether the National Symphony Orchestra might read the piece during their visit to campus in April. Dawson declined, citing the existence of only one set of parts. Letter from Childers to Dawson, November 21, 1934, William Levi Dawson Papers, series 1.

6. Robert Russa Moton, Principal's Annual Report, *The Tuskegee Institute Bulletin* XXV, no. 3 (July 1932), 5–6, Tuskegee University Archives.

7. *Tuskegee Normal and Industrial Institute Catalogue, 1930–31*, 73, Tuskegee University Archives.

8. *Tuskegee Normal and Industrial Institute Catalogue, 1931–32*, 116, Tuskegee University Archives.

9. Although he had been given the authority to dismiss whomever he liked, pianist Effie W. MacKerrow was the only member of the existing faculty whom Dawson did not retain.

10. *Tuskegee Normal and Industrial Institute Bulletin, 1934–35*, 156, Tuskegee University Archives.

11. *Tuskegee Normal and Industrial Institute Bulletin, 1931–32*, 135, Tuskegee University Archives. For a reference point concerning the $400 annual price tag: the U.S. government's National Resources Committee in 1938 issued a report stating, "In the rural South, more than half of the nonrelief Negro families had incomes of less than $500; more than nine-tenths of them had incomes under $1,000," National Resources Committee, "Consumer Incomes in the United States: Their Distribution in 1935–36," https://hdl.handle.net/2027/mdp.39015010864455.

12. Rampersad, *Ralph Ellison: A Biography*, 54–55.

13. For a discussion of Dawson's nurturing role in some students' lives, see Gwynne Kuhner Brown, "Gender in the Life," 759–60.

14. "Songfest Feature of Sunday Afternoon's Festivities," *Chicago Defender*, April 18, 1931, 2.

15. Booker T. Washington, *Character Building: Being Addresses Delivered on Sunday Evenings to the Students of Tuskegee Institute* (New York: Doubleday, Page & Co., 1902), 253.

16. "Pupils' Singing Was 'Something Fierce,'" *Boston Daily Globe*, March 9, 1903, 14.

17. Virginia Smith, "Choir Director: William Levi Dawson Made Tuskegee Singers Famous During 1930–1956 Period," *Phenix City and East Alabama Today*, November 4, 1976; "William L. Dawson: Guest Appearances," Tuskegee University Archives, box 027.005.

18. Floyd J. Calvin, "6,200 Thrill to Spirituals of Tuskegee Choir," *Pittsburgh Courier*, December 31, 1932; "William L. Dawson: Guest Appearances," Tuskegee University Archives, box 027.005.

19. Beulah Mitchell Hill, "Tuskegee Choir Makes Musical History at Wesley Memorial," *Atlanta World*, May 18, 1932; "William L. Dawson: Guest Appearances," Tuskegee University Archives, box 027.005.

20. Cy Caldwell, "Experiment on Sixth Street," *The Outlook*, February 1933, 44.

21. Brooks Atkinson, "The Play: Music Hall's Opening," *New York Times*, December 28, 1932.

22. Tuskegee University Archives, Box 027.

23. Calvin, "6,200 Thrill to Spirituals"; "William L. Dawson: Guest Appearances," Tuskegee University Archives, box 027.005.

24. "Radio City Presents Its First Broadcast," *New York Times*, December 26, 1932.

25. The *Voices of Millions* score is in the William Levi Dawson Papers, series 2, box 1, folder 1.

26. The information in this paragraph and the following is compiled from various newspaper clippings from 1933, mostly unlabeled, Tuskegee University Archives, box 027.002.

27. "Tuskegee Choir: Negro Group Gives Concert for Forum in Academy of Music," *Philadelphia Evening Bulletin*, February 10, 1933.

28. H. H., "Music," *New York Times*, February 10, 1933.

29. Graham, *Spirituals and the Birth of a Black Entertainment Industry*, 35–37, 72–73.

30. Irving Weil, "Music: Tuskegeeans at Carnegie," *New York Evening Journal*, February 1933, Tuskegee University Archives, box 027.002.

31. "Tuskegee Choir Offers Concert," *New York Amsterdam News*, February 15, 1933, Tuskegee University Archives, box 027.002.

32. "A Striking Contribution to Musical America," *American Business Survey* (April 1933), 24, William Levi Dawson Papers, series 9, box 69, folder 6.

33. Dawson's handwritten notes on legal pad, William Levi Dawson Papers, series 3, box 24, folder 6.

34. President's Annual Report to Board of Trustees, 1932–33, Tuskegee University Archives.

35. "Programs: 1950–1959," Tuskegee University Archives, box 027.004. The brochure predates Rothafel's death in 1936.

36. Alexander Basy to G. Lake Imes, n.d., William Levi Dawson Papers, series 1, box 1, folder 1.

37. Correspondence, n.d., William Levi Dawson Papers, series 1, box 1, folder 4.

38. Dawson to Robert Russa Moton, February 19, 1935, William Levi Dawson Papers, series 1.

39. G. Lake Imes to Dawson, n.d., William Levi Dawson Papers, series 1, box 1, folder 1.

40. The emphasis in Cecile's name is on the first syllable: more like "diesel" than "Lucille."

41. Dawson to Cecile Nicholson, n.d., William Levi Dawson Papers, series 1, box 8, folder 22.

42. David Lee Johnson, "The Contributions of William L. Dawson," 57, 82, 97–98.

43. Frederick D. Patterson, *Chronicles of Faith: The Autobiography of Frederick D. Patterson*, ed. Martia Graham Goodson (Tuscaloosa: University of Alabama Press, 1991).

44. President's Report to the Board, 1938–39, Tuskegee University Archives.

45. 1937–38 *Bulletin*, 121; 1938–39 *Bulletin*, 118, Tuskegee University Archives.

46. 1942–43 *Bulletin*, 148, Tuskegee University Archives.

47. Jackson, *Come Like the Benediction*, 9.

48. David Lee Johnson, "The Contributions of William L. Dawson," 136.

49. Pool, *American Composer Zenobia Powell Perry*, 93.

50. Clyde Owen Jackson, "Weaver of the Arts: The William Levi Dawson Interdisciplinary Method for Teaching Musically Illiterate Young Adult Students," lecture presented at Tuskegee University, September 21, 2001, Tuskegee University Archives.

51. Ibid., 11.

52. Marques L. A. Garrett is the leading scholar on what he terms "the non-idiomatic choral music of black composers." See https://www.mlagmusic.com/research/beyond-elijah-rock.

53. "$10,000 Broadcast by Tuskegee Choir Gives 'Bama Governor Spot," *New York Amsterdam News*, October 2, 1937, Tuskegee University Archives, box 027.001.

54. Sally Bell, "On the Air," *California Eagle*, October 14, 1937, Tuskegee University Archives, box 027.001.

55. Ibid.

56. James Edmund Boyack, "Tuskegee Choir Gets Enthusiastic Welcome," *Philadelphia Tribune*, October 28, 1937, Tuskegee University Archives, box 027.001.

57. Audio recording of Tuskegee Choir on the National Broadcasting Corporation, radio broadcast from Tuskegee, Alabama, October 10, 1937, William Levi Dawson Papers, series 11, LP8.

58. "$10,000 Broadcast by Tuskegee Choir..."

59. "Highlights in the Career of William L. Dawson," William Levi Dawson Papers, series 7, box 42, folder 2.

60. John H. Young III, "Tuskegee Choir Sings Amid Furor," *Pittsburgh Courier*, June 8, 1946, Tuskegee University Archives, box 027.001.

61. Ibid.

62. Felton, "No 'Honky Tonk Stuff...'"

63. Glenn Dillard Gunn, "Capacity Crowd Hears Concert by Tuskegee Choir," *Washington Times-Herald*, June 4, 1946, quoted in Malone, "William Dawson and the Tuskegee Choir," 22.

64. Typescript by G. Lake Imes, Tuskegee University Archives, box 027.001, "Biographical" folder.

65. The only exception, to be discussed in chapter 5, was his trip to Africa in 1952–53, which he said he would have taken regardless of whether Tuskegee Institute had granted him a sabbatical.

66. Meeting minutes of Tuskegee Institute Educational Council, January 15, 1954, Tuskegee University Archives microfilm.

67. Dawson, "Report from the Department of Music for the School Year 1953–1954," Tuskegee University Archives microfilm.

68. Ibid.

69. Ross Parmenter, "LP Choral History: Plainsong to Spirituals Offered on New Disks," *New York Times*, August 18, 1957, X9.

70. Thomas B. Sherman, "Classical Records: Mozart Magic," *St. Louis Post-Dispatch*, December 5, 1955.

71. Kurt List to Dorothy Barker, December 13, 1955, William Levi Dawson Papers, series 1, box 3, folder 9.

72. "Annual Report of the President 1954–55," 23, Tuskegee University Archives microfilm.

73. Dawson, "Interpretation of the Religious Folk-Songs," 11.

74. Ibid., 61.

75. Ibid., 61.

76. "Dawson Quits at Tuskegee," *Pittsburgh Courier*, October 1, 1955, William Levi Dawson Papers.

77. Dawson to Bill Trent Jr., February 14, 1955, William Levi Dawson Papers, series 9, box 69, folder 11.

78. Malone, *William Levi Dawson*, 73.

79. President Luther H. Foster, Report to the Tuskegee Institute Board of Trustees on the period from June 1 to September 30, 1955, Tuskegee University Archives.

80. Board of Trustees meeting Minutes, April 2, 1955, Tuskegee University Archives, microfilm 203ii.

81. Eugene Thamon Simpson, e-mail message to author, June 30, 2015.

82. McKinney Smith, "Famed Director of Choir Resigns," *Campus Digest*, October 14, 1955, William Levi Dawson Papers, series 9, box 69, folder 11.

83. Music Department Meeting Minutes, February 29, 1956, Tuskegee University Archives, microfilm 203a.

84. Program for Founder's Day Exercises at Tuskegee Institute, March 25, 1956, William Levi Dawson Papers, series 9, box 101, folder 4.

85. Eugene Thamon Simpson, e-mail message to author, June 14, 2014.

86. James G. Spady, "William L. Dawson and the Tuskegee Tradition," ca. 1989, William Levi Dawson Papers, series 1, box 8, folder 3.

Chapter 3. Vocal Music

1. There is ample quantitative and qualitative evidence to support the canonic status of Dawson's choral music among choir directors at HBCUs, and for Dawson's towering influence on other arrangers of African American religious folk songs; see Simmonds, "Jubilee," 48–53, 71–73, 100.

2. Hurston, "Spirituals and Neo-Spirituals," 473.

3. The analyses in this chapter are of the SATB versions of Dawson's arrangements. He created versions of many of his arrangements for other voice combinations, such as SSAA and TTBB. The differences among these are interesting but generally subtle.

4. Dawson, "Interpretation of the Religious Folk-Songs," 61.

5. *Feed-A My Sheep*, published in 1971, has a piano accompaniment, but it is an original composition with little stylistic resemblance to a folk song.

6. Work, *American Negro Songs and Spirituals*, 195. I am grateful to Sandra Jean Graham for the insight about the likelihood of interpolated syllables being part of oral tradition.

7. One was by Frederick Hall (1955); the other, by Robert W. Thygerson (1978), is discussed in chapter 5.

8. Eugene Thamon Simpson, *A Host of Angels*, 57.

9. James Kinchen, phone interview by the author, July 31, 2017.

10. Dett, *Religious Folk-Songs*, 88; Work, *American Negro Songs and Spirituals*, 128.

11. Floyd Jr., *The Power of Black Music*, 8.

12. Dawson, "Interpretation of the Religious Folk-Songs," 61.

13. Outwin, "William Dawson—Ithaca at Last…"

14. Montgomery, *Brothers, Sing On!*, 97–98.

15. Wyatt, "Composers Corner," 6.

Chapter 4. Instrumental Music

1. "Negro Composer Honored for Symphony," *Evening Public Ledger*, November 17, 1934, William Levi Dawson Papers, series 9, box 69, folder 6.

2. Leopold Stokowski to Governor B. M. Miller, March 22, 1933, http://scottsboroboys letters.as.ua.edu/items/show/505.

3. Wyatt, "Composers Corner," 6.

4. Leopold Stokowski to Dawson, telegram, November 1, 1934, William Levi Dawson Papers, series 1, box 1, folder 8.

5. In an inverse situation, Florence Price deleted the subtitle "Negro Symphony" from her Symphony in E Minor, "possibly because it might have suggested a programmatic work and limited the perception of the symphony's scope." Rae Linda Brown, "Lifting the Veil," xliii.

6. Dawson, interview by *The Sunday Show* (National Public Radio), 1982, William Levi Dawson Papers, series 11, box AV7, folder 20.

7. Dawson, audio recording of televised interview by James Hall, Houston, Texas, 1971, William Levi Dawson Papers, series 11, box AV3.

8. Pitts Sanborn, "Negro Music Played Here at Carnegie," *New York World-Telegram*, November 21, 1934, William Levi Dawson Papers, series 9, box 69, folder 6.

9. Mae Belle Thomas to Dawson, November 17, 1934, William Levi Dawson Papers, series 1, box 1, folder 13.

10. Samuel Chotzinoff, "Words and Music," *New York Post*, November 21, 1934, William Levi Dawson Papers, series 9, box 69, folder 6.

11. Leonard Liebling, "Native Musical Movement Stamped with the Strong Influence of Europe," *New York American*, November 25, 1934, William Levi Dawson Papers, series 9, box 69, folder 6.

12. Leonard Liebling, "Looking Backward," *New York American*, December 30, 1934, William Levi Dawson Papers, series 9, box 69, folder 6.

13. Winthrop Sargeant, "Music of the Day," *Brooklyn Daily Eagle*, n.d., William Levi Dawson Papers, series 9, box 69, folder 11.

14. "Symphonic Novelties Brighten Orchestral Fortnight," *Musical America*, December 16, 1934, 8; quoted in Shadle, *Antonín Dvořák's "New World Symphony,"* 159.

15. Locke, "Toward a Critique of Negro Music," 115.

16. Gwynne Kuhner Brown, "Whatever Happened to William Dawson's *Negro Folk Symphony*?," 444–47.

17. Correspondence between Dawson and Shawnee Press, William Levi Dawson Papers, series 3, box 28, folder 17.

18. Dawson, interview by *The Sunday Show*. My thanks to Jason Posnock for talking to me about the circumstances leading to the title change at Brevard.

19. NPR's Tom Huizenga listed the album among the best classical music releases of 2020, https://www.npr.org/sections/deceptivecadence/2020/12/21/947149286.

20. *Negro Folk Symphony* performances, Wise Music Classical, https://www.wisemusic classical.com/performances/search/work/27260/.

21. James Blachly, e-mail message to author, July 22, 2022.

22. See Rae Linda Brown, "Lifting the Veil"; Shadle, *Antonín Dvořák's New World Symphony*, 157–60; Catherine Parsons Smith, "The Afro-American Symphony and Its Scherzo," in *William Grant Still: A Study in Contradictions* (Berkeley: University of California Press, 2000), 129.

23. Antonín Dvořák, "Real Value of Negro Melodies," *New York Herald*, May 21, 1893.

24. Dawson had also encountered the symphony as a performer: the Largo movement was programmed by the Chicago Civic Orchestra during its 1927–28 season. My thanks to Frank Villella, director of the Rosenthal Archives of the Chicago Symphony, for this information.

25. Rae Linda Brown, "William Grant Still, Florence Price, and William Dawson"; John Andrew Johnson, "William Dawson, 'The New Negro,' and His Folk Idiom."

26. Burgett, "Vindication as a Thematic Principle," 29–31.

27. The 1934 program notes are provided as an appendix in Gwynne Kuhner Brown, "Whatever Happened to William Dawson's *Negro Folk Symphony*?," 452–53. Lawrence Gilman, "the annotator," credits Dawson with supplying the information in the notes.

28. George Jellinek, liner notes, *Negro Folk Symphony*, Decca DL 71077, 1963.

29. Jackson, "Weaver of the Arts."

30. Maxile, "Signs, Symphonies, Signifyin(g)," 128.

31. The other detailed analyses are John Andrew Johnson, "William Dawson, 'The New Negro,' and His Folk Idiom," 49–54, and Farrah, "Signifyin(g)," 129–54. Farrah's analysis is of the original, unrevised version. Briefer analytical comments appear in Rae Linda Brown, "William Grant Still, Florence Price, and William Dawson," 77–78, and in Gwynne Kuhner Brown, "Whatever Happened to William Dawson's *Negro Folk Symphony*?," 448–51.

32. The prominent use of the same motive in Robert Nathaniel Dett's oratorio *The Ordering of Moses* would seem to confirm the motive's origin in *Go Down, Moses*. The two works were composed during roughly the same period, and I have seen no evidence that the motivic similarity is anything but an astonishing coincidence.

33. Jellinek, liner notes, *Negro Folk Symphony*. All subsequent references to and quotations from the program are taken from Jellinek's liner notes, which are shorter than, but generally similar to, those in the 1934 Philadelphia Orchestra program.

34. The third movement provides a case study of the six "African and, by extension, Afro-American, conceptual approaches to the process of making music" discussed by Olly Wilson in "Black Music as an Art Form," 3.

35. Stan Voit, "Dawson Remembers Leopold Stokowski," *Tuskegee News*, September 22, 1977, William Levi Dawson Papers, series 9, box 69, folder 2.

36. *Negro Folk Symphony* piano score, William Levi Dawson papers, series 2, box 10, folder 4.

37. Dawson to John Lasher, draft, n.d. (ca. 1984), William Levi Dawson Papers, series 6, box 38, folder 3.

38. Yarbrough, "Critical Edition: Sonata for Violin and Piano."

39. "Deep River | Witness: American Spirituals and the Classical Music Tradition," Isabella Stewart Gardner Museum, March 25, 2021, https://youtu.be/4xSnHQozgic?t=353.

40. "Symphony in Black," *Nashville Tennessean*, January 2, 1933, William Levi Dawson Papers, series 9, box 69, folder 6.

41. Todd Harvey, "Alan Lomax Radio-Related Materials, 1939–1969: A Guide," 2006, http://www.loc.gov/static/collections/alan-lomax-manuscripts/documents/lomax_radio _master.pdf.

42. Most of the episode, including *A Negro Work Song*, can be heard in the online audio materials of Stone, *Listening to the Lomax Archive*.

43. Dawson to Thor Johnson, February 5, 1948, William Levi Dawson Papers, series 1, box 3, folder 6. Dawson does not encourage Johnson to program the piece.

44. It was performed by the Richmond Symphony Orchestra (1950), the Birmingham Symphony Orchestra (1951), and the Virginia Symphony Orchestra (1954). "Highlights in the Career of William L. Dawson," William Levi Dawson Papers, series 7, box 42, folder 2.

45. Stone, *Listening to the Lomax Archive*, 181.

Chapter 5. After Tuskegee

1. William and Cecile Dawson, interview by James Standifer.

2. Dawson interview, Philadelphia, October 1979.

3. Dawson, audio recording of televised interview by James Hall.

4. Dawson interview, Philadelphia, October 1979.

5. Dawson to Cecile Dawson, November 1952, William Levi Dawson Papers.

6. Dawson to Cecile Dawson, November 24, 1952, William Levi Dawson Papers.

7. Information about Dawson's time in Africa is drawn from "Africa, 1952–1953," William Levi Dawson Papers, box 30, folder 1.

8. Dawson to Cecile Dawson, December 13, 1952, William Levi Dawson Papers, series 1, box 9, folder 2.

9. Dawson, "Interpretation of the Religious Folk-Songs," 61.

10. On the role of Black musicians in U.S. cultural diplomacy during the Cold War, see Von Eschen, *Satchmo Blows up the World*, and especially Fosler-Lussier, *Music in America's Cold War Diplomacy*, chapter 4.

11. Arthur P. Whitaker, *Spain and Defense of the West: Ally and Liability* (New York: Harper & Brothers, 1961), 58–59.

12. Dawson to Cecile Dawson, July 23, 1956, William Levi Dawson Papers, series 1, box 9, folder 6.

13. Dawson to Cecile Dawson, July 27, 1956, William Levi Dawson Papers, series 1, box 9, folder 6.

14. Dawson, report to Robert D. Barton, American Embassy in Madrid, 1956, William Levi Dawson Papers, series 4, box 29, folder 6.

15. Dawson, travel journal kept in Spain, 1956, William Levi Dawson Papers, series 6, box 41, folder 13.

16. Dawson to Cecile Dawson, July 31, 1956, William Levi Dawson Papers, series 1, box 9, folder 6.

17. Malone, *William Levi Dawson*, 124.

18. Louis Nicholas, "Christmas Carol Service by Fisk Choir Outstanding," *Nashville Tennessean*, December 14, 1958, William Levi Dawson Papers, series 9, box 69, folder 5.

19. "Choir Closes Fisk Music, Art Festival," *The Nashville Banner*, April 28, 1959, William Levi Dawson Papers, series 9, box 69, folder 5.

20. Louis Nicholas, "Fisk Music, Art Festival Ends on Note of Acclaim," *Nashville Tennessean*, April 27, 1959, William Levi Dawson Papers, series 9, box 69, folder 5.

21. Audio recording of Dawson conducting Pearl High School Band in rehearsal, 1958 or 1959, William Levi Dawson Papers, series 11, box AV4.

22. Dawson to Neil A. Kjos Jr., April 29, 1984, William Levi Dawson Papers, series 3, box 25, folder 14.

23. Violet Johnson to Dawson, September 12, 1960; Maurice C. Whitney to Dawson, September 21, 1960, William Levi Dawson Papers, series 5, box 31, folder 4.

24. Dawson to Violet Johnson, September 17, 1960, William Levi Dawson Papers, series 5, box 31, folder 6.

25. Dawson to Violet Johnson, October 17, 1960, William Levi Dawson Papers, series 5, box 31, folder 6.

26. Dawson to Violet Johnson, October 18, 1960, William Levi Dawson Papers, series 5, box 31, folder 6.

27. Clyde Owen Jackson, "Weaver of the Arts."

28. Honorary Doctorate of Music, Tuskegee Institute, March 25, 1956, William Levi Dawson Papers, series 7, box 43, folder 24.

29. John Haberlen, interview with author, June 19, 2015, Atlanta.

30. Dawson, handwritten speech on choral conducting, William Levi Dawson Papers, series 4, box 29, folder 4.

31. Certificate, American Choral Directors Association, March 1975, William Levi Dawson Papers, series 7, box 43, folder 28.

32. Proceedings of the Symposium for Black Choral Directors, Glassboro State College, September 8, 1979. I am indebted to Eugene Thamon Simpson for this source.

33. Leslie Burrs, "Sundawn" (unpublished essay), 1986.

34. Among the inaccuracies: Dawson did not spend six years in Germany studying composition with Hugo Riemann (1849–1919).

35. Neil A. Kjos Music Company royalty statements, William Levi Dawson Papers, series 3, box 25.

36. David A. Donet to Dawson, July 23, 1987, William Levi Dawson Papers, series 3, box 27, folder 11.

37. Dawson, notes for letter to Curt Hansen, ca. 1985, William Levi Dawson Papers, series 3, box 27, folder 10.

38. Richard Friedman, *Birmingham News*, February 13, 1976, William Levi Dawson Papers, series 9, box 69, folder 2.

39. "Negro Composer Honored at Philadelphia Concert," *Nashville Tennessean*, November 14, 1934, William Levi Dawson Papers, series 1, box 1, folder 13.

40. Correspondence between Frederic Johnson and Albert E. DeRenzis, February-March 1978, William Levi Dawson Papers, series 3, box 28, folder 17.

41. Shawnee Press royalty payments, William Levi Dawson Papers, series 3, box 28, folder 18.

42. Dawson to Robert W. Thygerson, July 26, 1978, William Levi Dawson Papers, series 3, box 27, folder 2.

43. Haberlen, "William Dawson and the Copyright Act," 5.

44. William Levi Dawson Papers, series 3, boxes 23–25 contain many documents pertaining to this case.

45. William Krasilovsky, phone interview with author, June 24, 2014.

46. Charles Cronin, "Dawson v. Hinshaw Music," Music Copyright Infringement Resource, GW Law Blogs, https://blogs.law.gwu.edu/mcir/case/dawson-v-hinshaw-music/. I am grateful to Dr. Katherine Leo for her reassurance that Dawson's fight was not in vain.

47. Video recording of Dawson's 90th Birthday Celebration at Tuskegee University, September 24, 1989, William Levi Dawson Papers, series 11, DVD2.

48. Peggy Peterman, "His Work Was Music to Our Ears," *St. Petersburg (Fla.) Times*, June 5, 1990, Tuskegee University Archives, box 027.002.

49. Video recording of Dawson's 90th Birthday Celebration at Tuskegee University, September 24, 1989, William Levi Dawson Papers, series 11, DVD2.

50. William Levi Dawson Symposium at Emory University, March 3–5, 2005, https://wayback.archive-it.org/6324/20111129170415/http://larson.library.emory.edu/dawson/web/slideshow.

51. Jennifer Randolph, phone interview with author, July 14, 2016.

52. Bernice J. Reagon, "Way Out of No Way," in *William L. Dawson*, ed. Spady, 18.

Works

1. "William Dawson," Neil A. Kjos Music Company website, https://kjos.com/person/view?id=1462.

SELECT DISCOGRAPHY

Recordings Featuring Choral Music by Dawson

The Tuskegee Institute Choir Sings Spirituals. William L. Dawson, Ann Elliott, Otis Wright, Ann Moore, Georgia Scott, William H. Johnson. Westminster Recording Co. WN 18080, 1955.
The Spirituals of William Dawson. St. Olaf Choir, Anton Armstrong, Marvis Martin. St. Olaf Records E-2159, 1997.
Ev'ry Time I Feel the Spirit. Tuskegee University Golden Voices Concert Choir. Wayne A. Barr. 2006.

OUT IN THE FIELDS

Oakland Youth Orchestra, Robert Hughes. *The Black Composer in America*. Desto DC7107, 2006.

NEGRO FOLK SYMPHONY

American Symphony Orchestra, Leopold Stokowski. Decca DL 10077, 1963 (first release); Brunswick XA 4520, 1963; Varèse Sarabande VC 81056, 1978; MCA Classics MCAD2–9826A, 1989; Deutsche Grammophon 4776502, 2007.
Detroit Symphony Orchestra, Neeme Järvi. Chandos Records CHAN 9226, 1993 (first release); Chandos Records 9909, 2001.
ORF Vienna Radio Symphony Orchestra, Arthur Fagen. Naxos 8.559870, 2020.
Royal Scottish National Orchestra, Kellen Gray. *African American Voices*. Linn Records CKD699, 2022.
Seattle Symphony, Roderick Cox. Seattle Symphony Media SSM1027, 2023.
Philadelphia Orchestra, Yannick Néget-Séguin. Deutsche Grammophon 4865137, 2023.

William L. Dawson Playing Trombone

High Fever / Here Comes the Hot Tamale Man. Cookie's Gingersnaps. Okeh 8369, 1926.
Love Found You for Me. Cookie's Gingersnaps. Okeh 40675, 1926.
Messin' Around. Cookie's Gingersnaps. Okeh 8390, 1926.

Alligator Crawl / Brainstorm. "Doc" Cook and His 14 Doctors of Syncopation. Columbia 1298D, 1927.

Willie the Weeper / Slue-Foot. "Doc" Cook and His 14 Doctors of Syncopation. Columbia 1970D, 1927.

WORKS

Published

The list is arranged by first publication to avoid confusion with works that were revised and/or republished later. Works are for unaccompanied chorus unless marked by an asterisk. Most of Dawson's vocal music is currently available through Neil A. Kjos Music Co.[1]

Forever Thine, solo voice and piano, Tuskegee, 1920

Jump Back, Honey, Jump Back, text by Paul Laurence Dunbar, solo voice and piano, Wunderlichs Piano Co., 1923

King Jesus Is A-Listening, FitzSimons, 1925

I Couldn't Hear Nobody Pray, FitzSimons, 1926

My Lord, What a Mourning, FitzSimons, 1926

Jesus Walked This Lonesome Valley, piano accompaniment; version for solo voice, Remick, 1927

Talk About a Child That Do Love Jesus, piano accompaniment; version for solo voice, FitzSimons, 1927

You Got to Reap Just What You Sow, piano accompaniment; version for solo voice, Gamble Hinged, 1927

Out in the Fields, piano accompaniment; version for solo voice, Gamble Hinged, 1929

The Mongrel Yank (renamed *The Rugged Yank*), text by Allen Quade, piano accompaniment, Gamble Hinged, 1930

Oh, What a Beautiful City, Tuskegee Music Press, 1934

Soon Ah Will Be Done, Tuskegee Music Press, 1934

Ain'-A That Good News, Tuskegee Music Press, 1937

There Is a Balm in Gilead, Tuskegee Music Press, 1939

Ezekiel Saw de Wheel, Tuskegee Music Press, 1942

Steal Away, Tuskegee Music Press, 1942

Behold the Star, Tuskegee Music Press, 1946

Ev'ry Time I Feel the Spirit, Tuskegee Music Press, 1946

Hail Mary!, Tuskegee Music Press, 1946

Swing Low, Sweet Chariot, Tuskegee Music Press, 1946

Li'l Boy-Chile, Tuskegee Music Press, 1947

Mary Had a Baby, Tuskegee Music Press, 1947
There's a Lit'l' Wheel A-Turnin', Tuskegee Music Press, 1949
In His Care-O, Tuskegee Music Press, 1961
Zion's Walls, Tuskegee Music Press, 1961
I Wan' to Be Ready, Neil A. Kjos Music Co., 1967
Pilgrim's Chorus from "Tannhäuser" by Richard Wagner, Neil A. Kjos Music Co., 1968
*The Rugged Yank (originally *The Mongrel Yank*), text by Allen Quade, piano accompaniment, Neil A. Kjos Music Co., 1970
*Feed-A My Sheep, text by G. Lake Imes, piano accompaniment, Neil A. Kjos Music Co., 1971
*Slumber Song, text by Vernon N. Ray, piano accompaniment, Neil A. Kjos Music Co., 1974
*Before the Sun Goes Down, text by Edith Sanford Tillotson, piano accompaniment, arrangement of *Londonderry Air*, Neil A. Kjos Music Co., 1978
*Dorabella, piano accompaniment, Neil A. Kjos Music Co., 1981
*Negro Folk Symphony, orchestra, G. Schirmer, 2023 (first completed in 1929; revised after 1952; critical performance edition by Gwynne Kuhner Brown, 2023)

Unpublished (selected)

Manuscripts of the works below are held in the William Levi Dawson Papers in the Stuart A. Rose Manuscript, Archives, and Rare Book Library, Emory University. Unfinished pieces, school exercises, and hymnlike SATB settings are not included.

UNACCOMPANIED CHORUS

All Over God's Hebum!
Go Tell It On the Mountain
Hallelujah!, 1931
I Want to Be Ready
The Journey to Calvary
Mary Had a Chile

ACCOMPANIED CHORUS

Break, Break, Break, versions with piano and with orchestra
Out in the Fields, versions for chorus and wind ensemble, chorus and orchestra, solo voice and orchestra
Talk about a Child That Do Love Jesus for soprano solo, SATB chorus, piano, and organ

SOLO VOICE AND PIANO

Dawn (text by Paul Laurence Dunbar)
Go to Sleep (Lullaby)
Good Night (text by Paul Laurence Dunbar)
The Mongrel Yank (text by Allen Quade)

SOLO/CHAMBER

Ansietà (Anxiety) / Ansioso (Anxiety) / Interlude for piano (manuscripts of same piece with different titles)

Konju-Raku for trombone and piano

Romance for violin and piano, 1922

Romance in A for violin, cello, and piano

Sonata in A for violin and piano; Largo movement also arranged for piano trio and string quartet

FOR LARGE ENSEMBLE

Adagietto for string orchestra

Dance: Juba, concert band arrangement of movement from R. Nathaniel Dett, *In the Bottoms Suite*

A Negro Work Song for orchestra, 1940

Poème Érotique, concert band arrangement of piano piece by Melville Charlton

SOURCES AND BIBLIOGRAPHY

Archives

William Levi Dawson Papers. Stuart A. Rose Manuscript, Archives, and Rare Book Library. Emory University, Atlanta.
Tuskegee University Archives. Tuskegee, Alabama.

Secondary Sources

Abromeit, Kathleen A. *Spirituals: A Multidisciplinary Bibliography for Research and Performance*. MLA Index and Bibliography 38. Middleton, WI: Music Library Association and A-R Editions, 2015.
Anderson, James D. *The Education of Blacks in the South, 1860–1935*. Chapel Hill: The University of North Carolina Press, 1988.
Baldwin, Davarian. *Chicago's New Negroes: Modernity, the Great Migration, and Black Urban Life*. Chapel Hill: University of North Carolina Press, 2007.
Baxa, Philip C., and M. William Krasilovsky. "Dawson v. Hinshaw Music, Inc.: The Fourth Circuit Revisits Arnstein and the 'Intended Audience' Test." *Fordham Intellectual Property, Media and Entertainment Law Journal* no. 1/2 (1991): 91–115.
Bond, Horace Mann. *Negro Education in Alabama: A Study in Cotton and Steel*. Tuscaloosa: The University of Alabama Press, 1994.
Brown, Gwynne Kuhner. "Gender in the Life and Legacy of William Levi Dawson." *Journal of the American Musicological Society* 73, no. 3 (Fall 2020): 754–63.
Brown, Gwynne Kuhner. "Whatever Happened to William Dawson's *Negro Folk Symphony*?" *Journal of the Society for American Music* 6, no. 4 (November 2012): 433–56.
Brown, Rae Linda. "Lifting the Veil: The Symphonies of Florence B. Price." In *Florence Price: Symphonies Nos. 1 and 3*, edited by Rae Linda Brown and Wayne Shirley, xv–lii. Music of the United States of America, vol. 19. Middleton, WI: A-R Editions, 2008.
Brown, Rae Linda. *The Heart of a Woman: The Life and Music of Florence B. Price*. Edited by Guthrie P. Ramsey. Urbana: University of Illinois Press, 2020.
Brown, Rae Linda. "William Grant Still, Florence Price, and William Dawson: Echoes of the Harlem Renaissance." In *Black Music in the Harlem Renaissance*, edited by Samuel A. Floyd, Jr., 71–86. Knoxville: University of Tennessee Press, 1990.

Buckner, Reginald T. "Rediscovering Major N. Clark Smith." *Music Educators Journal* 71, no. 6 (April 1985): 36–42.

Burgett, Paul. "Vindication as a Thematic Principle in the Writings of Alain Locke on the Music of Black Americans." In *Black Music in the Harlem Renaissance*, edited by Samuel A. Floyd Jr., 29–40. Knoxville: University of Tennessee Press, 1990.

Cazort, Jean, and Constance Hobson. "Hazel Harrison: Première Pianiste." *Black Music Research Journal* no. 10/1 (Spring 1990): 113–17.

Citron, Marcia J. "Gender, Professionalism and the Musical Canon." *The Journal of Musicology* 8, no. 1 (Winter 1990): 102–17.

Crawley, Kaylina Madison. "John Wesley Work III: Arranger, Preserver, and Historian of African American Traditional Music." PhD diss., University of Kentucky, 2021.

Dawson, William L. "Interpretation of the Religious Folk-Songs of the American Negro." *Etude* (March 1955): 11, 58, 61. https://digitalcommons.gardner-webb.edu/etude/92.

Dawson, William, and Cecile Dawson. Post-1967 interview by James Standifer. *Nathaniel C. Standifer Video Archive of Oral History: Black American Musicians.* http://www.umich.edu/~afroammu/standifer/dawson.html.

Dett, R. Nathaniel. *Religious Folk-Songs of the Negro as Sung at Hampton Institute.* Hampton, VA: Hampton Institute Press, 1927.

Dett, R. Nathaniel. *The R. Nathaniel Dett Reader: Essays on Black Sacred Music.* Edited by Jon Michael Spencer. Durham, NC: Duke University Press, 1991.

Du Bois, W. E. B., Henry Louis Gates Jr., and Terri Hume Oliver. *The Souls of Black Folk: Authoritative Text, Contexts, Criticism.* Norton Critical Edition. New York: W. W. Norton & Company, 1999.

Ege, Samantha. "Composing a Symphonist: Florence Price and the Hand of Black Women's Fellowship." *Women & Music* 24, no. 1 (2020): 7–27.

Ellison, Ralph. "Homage to William L. Dawson." In *Living with Music: Ralph Ellison's Jazz Writings*, edited by Robert G. O'Meally, 133–38. New York: Modern Library, 2001.

Enck, Henry S. "Tuskegee Institute and Northern White Philanthropy: A Case Study in Fund Raising, 1900–1915." *The Journal of Negro History* 65, no. 4 (Autumn 1980): 336–48.

Epstein, Dena. *Sinful Tunes and Spirituals: Black Music to the Civil War.* Urbana: University of Illinois Press, 1977, 2003.

Evans, Arthur L. "The Development of the Negro Spiritual as Choral Art Music by Afro-American Composers with an Annotated Guide to the Performance of Selected Spirituals." PhD diss., University of Miami, 1972.

Farrah, Scott David. "Signifyin(g): A Semiotic Analysis of Symphonic Works by William Grant Still, William Levi Dawson, and Florence B. Price." PhD diss., Florida State University, 2007.

Floyd, Samuel A., Jr. *The Power of Black Music: Interpreting Its History from Africa to the United States.* New York: Oxford University Press, 1995.

Floyd, Samuel A., Jr. "Ring Shout! Literary Studies, Historical Studies, and Black Music Inquiry." *Black Music Research Journal* 22 (2002): 49–70.

Floyd, Samuel A., Jr. "The Negro Renaissance: Harlem and Chicago Flowerings." In *The Black Chicago Renaissance*, edited by Darlene Clark Hine, John McCluskey, and Marshanda A. Smith, 21–43. Urbana: University of Illinois Press, 2012.

Fosler-Lussier, Danielle. *Music in America's Cold War Diplomacy*. Oakland: University of California Press, 2015.

Graham, Sandra Jean. *Spirituals and the Birth of a Black Entertainment Industry*. Urbana: University of Illinois Press, 2018.

Haberlen, John B. "William Dawson and the Copyright Act." *Choral Journal* 3 (1983): 5–8.

Harris, Carl G., Jr. "Three Schools of Black Choral Composers and Arrangers 1900–1970." *The Choral Journal* 14 (April 1974): 11–18.

Harris, Carl Gordon, Jr. "A Study of Characteristic Stylistic Trends Found in Choral Works of a Selected Group of Afro-American Composers and Arrangers." DMA thesis, University of Missouri-Kansas City, 1972.

Hash, Philip M. "The Frederick Neil Innes / Conn National School of Music, 1915–1932." *Journal of Band Music* 56, no. 1 (Fall 2020): 30–58.

Helton, Caroline, and Emery Stephens. "Singing Down the Barriers: Encouraging Singers of All Racial Backgrounds to Perform Music by African American Composers." In *Scholarship of Multicultural Teaching and Learning*, edited by A. T. Miller, 73–79. San Francisco: Jossey-Bass, 2007.

Hood, Marcia Mitchell. "William Levi Dawson and His Music: A Teacher's Guide to Interpreting His Choral Spirituals." DMA diss., University of Alabama, 2004.

Horowitz, Joseph. *Dvořák's Prophecy and the Vexed Fate of Black Classical Music*. New York: W. W. Norton, 2022.

Huff, Vernon Edward. "William Levi Dawson: An Examination of Selected Letters, Speeches, and Writings." DMA diss., Arizona State University, 2013.

Huff, Vernon. "William Levi Dawson's Life in Speeches, Letters, and Writings." *The Choral Journal* 55, no. 1 (2014): 65–70.

Huff, Vernon. "William Levi Dawson (1899–1990): Reexamination of a Legacy." *The Choral Journal* 59, no. 10 (2019): 20–33.

Hurston, Zora Neale. "Spirituals and Neo-Spirituals." In *The New Negro: Readings on Race, Representation, and African American Culture, 1892–1938*, edited by Henry Louis Gates Jr. and Gene Andrew Jarrett, 473–75. Princeton: Princeton University Press, 2007.

Jackson, Clyde Owen. *Come Like the Benediction: A Tribute to Tuskegee Institute and Other Essays*. Smithtown, NY: Exposition Press, 1981.

Johnson, David Lee. "The Contributions of William L. Dawson to the School of Music at Tuskegee Institute and to Choral Music." EdD diss., University of Illinois at Urbana-Champaign, 1987.

Johnson, John Andrew. "William Dawson, 'The New Negro,' and His Folk Idiom." *Black Music Research Journal* 19, no. 1 (Spring 1999): 43–60.

Kenney, William Howland. *Chicago Jazz: A Cultural History, 1904–1930*. New York: Oxford University Press, 1993.

Leo, Katherine M. "Musical Expertise and the 'Ordinary' Listener in Federal Copyright Law." *Music & Politics* 13, no. 1 (Winter 2019): 1–19.

Locke, Alain. "Toward a Critique of Negro Music." In *The Critical Temper of Alain Locke: A Selection of His Essays on Art and Culture*, edited by Jeffrey C. Stewart, 109–15. New York: Garland, 1983.

Lovell, John, Jr. *Black Song: The Forge and the Flame*. New York: The Macmillan Company, 1972.

Lowe, Donald R. "Carl Busch: Danish-American Music Educator." *Journal of Research in Music Education* 31, no. 2 (1983): 85–92.

Lush, Paige Clark. "Music and Identity in Circuit Chautauqua: 1904–1932." PhD diss., University of Kentucky, 2009.

Malone, Mark Hugh. "William Levi Dawson: American Music Educator." PhD diss., Florida State University, 1981.

Malone, Mark Hugh. "William Dawson and the Tuskegee Choir." *Choral Journal* 30, no. 8 (March 1990): 17–23.

Malone, Mark Hugh. *William Levi Dawson: American Music Educator*. American Made Music. Jackson: University Press of Mississippi, 2023.

Maxile, Horace J., Jr. "Signs, Symphonies, Signifyin(g): African-American Cultural Topics as Analytical Approach to the Music of Black Composers." *Black Music Research Journal* 28, no. 1 (Spring 2008): 123–38.

Maxile, Horace J., Jr. "Zenobia Powell Perry's *Homage* for William Levi Dawson." *Journal of the American Musicological Society* 73, no. 3 (Fall 2020): 763–70.

McGinty, Doris Evans. "'As Large as She Can Make It': The Role of Black Women Activists in Music, 1880–1945." In *Cultivating Music in America: Women Patrons and Activists since 1860*, edited by Ralph P. Locke and Cyrilla Barr, 214–36. Berkeley: University of California Press, 1997.

McMillan, William Robert. "The Choral Music of William Dawson." DA diss., University of Northern Colorado, 1991.

Melnick, Ross. *American Showman: Samuel "Roxy" Rothafel and the Birth of the Entertainment Industry, 1908–1935*. New York: Columbia University Press, 2012.

Montgomery, Bruce. *Brothers, Sing On!: My Half-Century around the World with the Penn Glee Club*. Philadelphia: University of Pennsylvania Press, 2005.

Newland, Marti. "Sounding 'Black': An Ethnography of Racialized Vocality at Fisk University." PhD diss., Columbia University, 2014.

Pool, Jeannie Gayle. *American Composer Zenobia Powell Perry*. Lanham, MD: Scarecrow, 2009.

Rampersad, Arnold. *Ralph Ellison: A Biography*. New York: Alfred A. Knopf, 2007.

Rampersad, Arnold. "Ralph Ellison at Tuskegee." *Journal of Blacks in Higher Education* 56 (Summer 2007): 59–67.

Roach, Hildred. *Black American Music: Past and Present*. 2nd ed. Malabar, FL: Krieger, 1992.

Russell, Ralph Anthony. "A Black Composer Speaks: William Levi Dawson." In *Black Lives: Essays in African American Biography*, edited by James L. Conyers Jr., 110–16. Armonk, NY: M.E. Sharpe, 1999.

Schenbeck, Lawrence. *Racial Uplift and American Music, 1878–1943*. Jackson: University Press of Mississippi, 2012.

Shadle, Douglas W. *Antonín Dvořák's "New World Symphony."* New York: Oxford University Press, 2021.

Simmonds, Kevin M. "Jubilee: The Place of Negro Spirituals as Perceived by Choir Directors at Historically Black Colleges and Universities." PhD diss., University of South Carolina, 2005.

Simpson, Anne Key. *Follow Me: The Life and Music of R. Nathaniel Dett*. Metuchen, NJ: Scarecrow Press, 1993.

Simpson, Eugene Thamon. *A Host of Angels*. West Conshohocken, PA: Infinity Publishing, 2010.

Smith, Catherine Parsons. *William Grant Still*. Urbana: University of Illinois Press, 2008.

Snyder, Jean E. *Harry T. Burleigh: From the Spiritual to the Harlem Renaissance*. Urbana: University of Illinois Press, 2016.

Southern, Eileen. *The Music of Black Americans: A History*. 3rd ed. New York: Norton, 1997.

Spady, James G., ed. *William L. Dawson: A Umum Tribute and a Marvelous Journey*. Philadelphia: Creative Artists' Workshop, 1981.

Spencer, Jon Michael. *The New Negroes and Their Music: The Success of the Harlem Renaissance*. Knoxville: University of Tennessee Press, 1997.

Stone, Jonathan W. *Listening to the Lomax Archive: The Sonic Rhetorics of African American Folksong in the 1930s*. Ann Arbor: University of Michigan Press, 2021. https://doi.org/10.3998/mpub.9871097.

Tick, Judith. *Ruth Crawford Seeger: A Composer's Search for American Music*. New York: Oxford University Press, 1997.

Von Eschen, Penny M. *Satchmo Blows up the World: Jazz Ambassadors Play the Cold War*. Cambridge: Harvard University Press, 2004.

Wallace, James A. "The Choral Tradition at Historically Black Colleges and Universities in Alabama, 1880–1940." DMA thesis, University of Cincinnati College-Conservatory of Music, 1998.

Washington, Booker T. *Up from Slavery: An Autobiography*. New York: Doubleday, 1901.

Wilkerson, Isabel. *The Warmth of Other Suns: The Epic Story of America's Great Migration*. New York: Random House, 2010.

Wilkins, Roy, with Tom Mathews. *The Autobiography of Roy Wilkins: Standing Fast*. New York: Viking Press, 1982.

Williams, Lea E. "The United Negro College Fund in Retrospect: A Search for Its True Meaning." *The Journal of Negro Education* 49, no. 4 (1980): 363–72.

Wilson, Olly. "Black Music as an Art Form." *Black Music Research Journal* 3 (1983): 1–22.

Wilson, Olly. "Composition From the Perspective of the African-American Tradition." *Black Music Research Journal* 16 (1996): 44–51.

Work, John W. *American Negro Songs and Spirituals*. New York: Crown, 1940.

Wyatt, Lucius R. "Composers Corner: William L. Dawson at 85." *Black Music Research Newsletter* 8, no. 1 (Fall 1985): 5–7.

Yarbrough, David Y. "Critical Edition: Sonata for Violin and Piano by William Levi Dawson." DMA diss., Peabody Conservatory of Music, 1999.

INDEX

GWYNNE KUHNER BROWN is a professor of music at the University of Puget Sound.

The University of Illinois Press
is a founding member of the
Association of University Presses.

—————————————————

University of Illinois Press 1325
South Oak Street Champaign, IL
61820-6903
www.press.uillinois.edu